THE WORMHOLE CRISIS

THE
WORMHOLE
CRISIS

A NOVEL OF TIME TRAVEL

Book Two of the
Wormhole Adventures

Russell F. Moran

The Wormhole Crisis

Coddington Press

Copyright © 2021 by Russell F. Moran

Printed in the United States of America

ISBN: 978-1-7338872-8-1

Covers and text design by LuAnn T. Palazzo.

www.morancom.com

DEDICATION

This book is dedicated to the
men and women of science.

FOREWORD

The Wormhole Crisis, a Novel of Time Travel, is the sequel to *The Wormhole Gang,* and is Book Two of *The Wormhole Adventures.* Our old friends, Ashley Patterson and her husband Jack Thurber are on yet another adventure. You may remember them from *The Gray Ship,* where they met and fell in love.

Their adventures continued with *The Thanksgiving Gang, The Skies of Time, The Keepers of Time, The Wormhole Gang,* and now with this book, *The Wormhole Crisis.* They are two of my favorite characters, and I think of them as old friends. As I wrote this book, we took a lot of adventures together. I hope you will see them that way too.

You will find a **Cast of Characters** after the last chapter of the book. It can be frustrating to come across a character on page 150, who you first met on page 20, especially if you've put the book down for a few days. I've seen this done in Russian literature, and I happily add a cast of characters to *The Wormhole Crisis* as well as my other books.

THE WORMHOLE CRISIS

A NOVEL OF TIME TRAVEL

Book Two of the
Wormhole Adventures

Russell F. Moran

Coddington Press
Islip, NY

Chapter 1

J ack, what just happened? I thought we were done with this shit."

"I don't need to tell you what happened, Ashley, because you know as well as me what we just went through. We may not like the idea, but it's obvious that we're no longer in the same time we were two minutes ago. We've travelled through a wormhole."

Jack's right, as usual, but I wish he wasn't. We were enjoying a meal with friends on the *Queen Mary 2* when it happened. Jack and I couldn't have been happier to be aboard the QM2, the ship on which we spent our honeymoon not long ago. We boarded the *Queen* this afternoon at Clinton Wharf, Pier 12 in Brooklyn. Jack had secured us a huge stateroom on the top deck with beautiful ocean views. Jack likes to do things big. The ship was steaming off the south shore of Long Island, heading for Europe. We looked through the large window in the dining room and admired the mansions of East Hampton where Jack wants to buy a beach House. You would think that our six-bedroom townhouse on Fifth Avenue and our huge lake house in Connecticut would be enough, but no, my husband, who makes a fortune with his book writing and publishing business, likes to buy pretty things. Because of Jack's many talents, we're up to our eyeballs in money.

But money can't save us from what we just went through. The bright sky suddenly went dark and we felt a sharp rumbling beneath us as if we were steaming over logs. In exactly two minutes, the daylight returned, and the rumbling stopped. We can try to deny it, but Jack was right. We knew what happened because we'd done this before. We went through a *wormhole*, a goddam wormhole, a time portal to a different era. Yes, we traveled through time, as bizarre as that sounds. The mansions of Long Island disappeared, and we looked at a forest bordered by a large field of grass. I saw a huge herd of bison. Yes, fucking bison—on suburban Long Island!

The irony of what happened made me dizzy. We were on the *Queen Mary 2* to celebrate the end of a crisis, one that Jack and I were deeply involved in. President Blake had declared a National State of Emergency in response to the problem, and assigned us to work with the CIA. So, there we were on the *QM2* celebrating the end of a catastrophe the President aptly named, *The Wormhole Crisis*. A wormhole, which scientists call an Einstein-Rosen bridge, is a portal in time, sort of like a split in time itself, from one age to another. Slip through a wormhole, and you've traveled through time. A wormhole, a rare phenomenon, had always been thought of as a natural, if strange, occurrence. But government scientists, mainly at the Department of Defense, recently discovered that wormholes can be created on the earth by instruments on a satellite. DOD enrolled the CIA in the effort, and focused the investigation on terrorism. So, wormholes can be man-made, not only an accident of nature. Yes, somebody can make it happen, as insane as that sounds. President Blake assigned Jack and me to work with the CIA to end man-made time travel, the most horrifying crisis the country had ever faced. I mean, shit, life throws enough at you, but at least you can count on knowing where you are in time and place. That dependable certainty goes out the friggin window with time travel. The President named the mission, appropriately enough, *Operation Wormhole Kill*, the purpose of which was to end the crisis. With the help of the CIA, Jack and I put an end to the strange phenomenon. Or we thought we did.

It's a bitch to think you put something bad behind you, only to discover it's still staring you in the face. Looks like we celebrated too soon.

My name is Ashley Patterson, and at age 39, I'm the youngest Admiral in the United States Navy.

My husband, Jack, the famous author and publisher, is a captain in the Naval Reserve. He tells me that I'm the prettiest admiral in the Navy, not only the youngest. Jack throws sweet compliments my way like he throws around money. I've gotten some big things done in my life, but marrying Jack was my number one accomplishment. Until I met Jack, I really didn't know what love was all about. I love him to pieces. I have no idea what that means, but somehow that goofy phrase captures my feelings about him.

We were traveling with our good friends, Jenny Blake and her new husband, Mike Jackson, two people that Jack and I think of as dear best friends, more like brother and sister. After what just happened, they were as upset as Jack and me. Jenny is a cousin of Matt Blake, President of the United States. We met Jenny and Mike on a recent bizarre time travel journey when I was commanding officer of the *USS Intrepid*, an old, decommissioned *Essex* Class aircraft carrier that became the major part of the *Intrepid Sea, Air, and Space Museum* in Manhattan. A lot of people, when they think of the docks of the West Side, picture the *Intrepid,* one of Manhattan's most famous landmarks.

Admiral Pete Wetherill is the Director of Naval Personnel and is well-known for his public relations ideas. He came up with the idea for me, the Navy's youngest admiral, to take command of the *USS Intrepid* for a three-month "deployment." His thinking was that it would help the museum with its marketing efforts and would also be a great public relations stunt and recruiting effort for the Navy. Hey, why not? I couldn't have been prouder to serve on a ship with such an illustrious career. During that three-month assignment, I was more like a museum curator than a ship captain, and I loved every minute of it. I've always been a big fan of history and the *Intrepid* deployment was perfect for me. As he often does, Jack took time off from managing his publishing company and accompanied me as my Chief of Staff. Over the years, Jack put together a talented team of executives, enabling him to turn over the management reins to others. Jack and I arrange our lives to spend as much time together as possible. To say that we're in love doesn't quite describe our relationship. And even though my position requires me to be a pain in the ass at times, I know he loves me too, despite my talent for getting on people's nerves. I also have a somewhat salty tongue. No shit.

The three-month assignment was a largely ceremonial post, and, because I was with Jack, it was a lot of fun. After my stint on the museum ship *Intrepid,* President Blake promoted me to Fleet Admiral, the senior position in the Navy, the first such appointment since Admiral Halsey in 1945, and the first woman to hold the post. He also named me as Chairwoman of the Joint Chiefs of Staff, the first woman to hold that job. Safe to say that President Blake thinks a lot of me. I must admit that

I do know what I'm doing, and when given an assignment I get it done. I don't just give orders, I take them. They trained me well at Annapolis. He then freaked me out when he put me in charge of putting an end to man-made time travel.

So, along with the CIA and Jack, I became the honcho of *Operation Wormhole Kill*. I must admit that I felt like hot stuff. But I was also scared shitless. People look at me and see a highly accomplished leader. They would be surprised to know that in my quiet moments I wallow in self-doubt. When I was a kid, my friends called me *Splashy* for fun. Little did they know that their little friend hated herself most of the time. Sometimes I think that my public persona is a big act. Ashley Patterson, the tall, beautiful admiral who has a hard time getting out of bed in the morning because I'm gripped with self-doubt. I'm not always that way, but more than I like. I really need to get my shit together. Being married to Jack helps. He puts up with my hang-ups, and even gently reminds me that I have a lot to be proud of. Jack is the man, *my* man. Besides being insanely handsome, Jack is the sexiest man imaginable. Have I mentioned how much I love him?

The idea of capturing the wormhole-creating satellite was hatched by our good friend, Jenny Blake, who was also the *Intrepid* Museum's History Department Director. Besides being brilliant, Jenny is a sweetheart of a human being, 32 years old and stunningly pretty. So, *Space Shuttle Atlantis* captured a terrorist satellite that had been creating wormholes on earth, fulfilling its mission. Yes, the satellite was captured, but, from the rumbling and light show we just experienced, we realized that the plan obviously didn't work as it was supposed to. Jack and I have been through this before, and so have Jenny and Mike.

This shit is getting old.

Chapter 2

M ike Jackson is Jenny's husband and one of the volunteers at the museum. They're both lieutenant commanders in the Naval Reserve and are now on active duty, having recently received promotions directly from President Blake, Jenny's cousin. In their civilian lives, Jenny and Mike are both professors at Columbia University. When Jack and I first met them, only the four of us were aboard, even though the *Intrepid* was steaming in the middle of the ocean at full speed. We never did figure it out what happened, other than the stark reality that we had traveled through time. We woke up that morning, expecting to see the glistening towers of mid-town Manhattan. Instead, our dock-bound museum ship was charging through the open ocean at full speed with nobody at the controls and with no discernible source of power. Time travel is weird, no getting around it.

Shortly after we got underway on the *Intrepid,* I noticed that Jenny and Mike were quite fond of each other, constantly at each other's sides and often holding hands. Sometimes serving as a volunteer has unexpected side benefits, such as a romance with a fellow volunteer. Jenny can best be described as stunning, with her pale blue eyes, natural blond hair, and a shapely athletic figure. Not only is she beautiful, she's also one of the kindest people I've ever met. If Jenny can think of something to help you with, you don't need to ask, she'll figure it out. Mike is an inch taller than Jenny and, with his wavy light brown hair and fit physique, is Hollywood handsome. They're both young at age 32. Jenny would be amazed to know that her Commanding Officer (me) actually looks to her for inspiration.

As a ship captain, I'm empowered to perform marriages, and at their request, I did just that. Typically, it was Jack's idea, which he announced right after Mike proposed marriage in front of us on the bridge. Besides being gorgeous, my Jack is an incurable romantic. It was a moment I'll never forget. Mike took a string from his pocket, which he always carries in case he needs to tie something. Professor Mike is an attentive sailor. He knelt down on one knee in front of Jenny, tied the string around her finger, and asked for her hand in marriage. I almost broke down in tears at Mike's sweet gesture. It was like something out of a Harlequin romance. The lovely little wedding ceremony almost made our strange time travel voyage enjoyable. I read the ceremony off my cellphone, which I had saved for occasions like this. Over the years I've officiated at six seagoing weddings. I may be a combat-ready senior naval officer but performing a wedding ceremony is one of my favorite tasks. To bring two lovers together in marriage is a gift from God. Jack served as best man, and even though I officiated, I was Jenny's maid of honor. Time travel sometimes requires amended traditions, especially because the wedding ceremony consisted of only four people. Mike and Jenny are now husband and wife, and I'm happy to say I made it happen. I love those two. Along with Jack, they make my hidden life of self-doubt tolerable.

So, the four of us steamed on the *Intrepid* through the ocean, having no idea where we were because all our navigational instruments were inoperable. On a clear, starlit night, we finally got an accurate celestial fix and determined that we were near England. How the hell we wound up near England was one of our unanswered questions. And we had plenty of questions. We had not only traveled through time but through physical space itself. I mean, holy shit, last I checked we were steaming off Long Island, New York. Have I mentioned that time travel is strange?

Jenny faced the window and pointed to the sky off our starboard side. We could see a squadron of old fighter aircraft. Jenny trained her binoculars on the flight of planes.

"They're F6F Grumman Hellcats," Jenny said. "They're ours, but what year are we in? Obviously, we aren't in the 19th Century."

Jenny the historian knows her stuff, and takes her research seriously, including aircraft identification.

I had set the radio to monitor all channels in case somebody wanted to get in touch with us. Please, God, make that happen.

One of the planes dropped in altitude and circled above us.

"Lima Juliette, Lima Juliette, this is U.S. Navy flight number 216, come in please."

Jenny looked at me and said, "Lima Juliette was the call sign for the *Intrepid* in World War II." My God, this lady knows her history.

I decided that our little group deserved a name, so, while we were on the *Intrepid*, I dubbed us *The Wormhole Gang*. Pretty appropriate name for four people on an old aircraft carrier that suddenly found itself a few decades in the past, no? Jenny, Mike, and Jack love the name I chose for our little group and are proud to be *Wormhole Gangsters*.

So, fast forward to the present. Here we are on the *Queen Mary 2*, a beautiful ocean liner, four people, along with 2,000 passengers and crew, with our minds in the sky and our heads up our asses.

The cruise we're on now is a celebration of the successful flight of the space shuttle, *Atlantis*, the first such flight in nine years. The mission was to capture a wormhole-creating satellite, no small fete. The propeller heads at the Defense Department discovered that a satellite can be designed to aim a high intensity energy beam at the earth. That beam can create a wormhole. But it gets worse. It can also detonate a bomb that it's aimed at. Definitely a scary power. President Blake had declared a National State of Emergency because he recognized what a threat man-made time travel could be. The scheme could literally reverse the world's reality. One of life's certainties, assuming you're conscious and mentally sound, is knowing where you are, in time and in physical space. Wormholes change all that. Slip through a wormhole and your world is suddenly different from the one you left.

The phone in our stateroom rang. It was the QM2's captain, Bill Westerbeke. We had dinner with him the night before and became fast friends. He was flabbergasted with our time travel stories. A few minutes ago, he was freaked out once again, suddenly finding that he too, was a time traveler. Non-time travelers are easily blown away the first time they do it. Can you blame them? I mean there you are handling the everyday *yada-yada* of life, and suddenly you're in a different world. Captain Bill asked to meet us in his office, and he requested that Jenny and Mike be there as well.

We walked into his office on the top deck, which, as you would guess with the *Queen Mary 2*, was quite large with a fabulous view of the ocean. I decided we should wear our Navy uniforms to help make the meeting more official. I didn't *order* the others to wear their uniforms, I simply suggested it. That's the way it is with me and *The Gang,* my three favorite people in the world. Although I'm an Admiral and the Commanding Officer, I don't give them orders, I make suggestions. And my wonderful *Gang* always salutes and follows my "suggestions."

Captain Bill showed us to our seats.

"Ashley and Jack, I'm simply amazed with you two as well as Jenny and Mike. You four are probably the world's experts on time travel. My God, you even call yourselves *The Wormhole Gang,* a perfectly apt name for your team. You folks took the strange phenomenon of time travel from the dust bins of science fiction and showed the world that it's the real thing, strange but real. I almost think I should give over command of the *Queen* to you and your *Wormhole Gang,* Ashley."

"You flatter us, Captain Bill," I said, "but we're more than confident to have you at the wheel. Please consider us your full-time consultants. We do know a bit about time travel, pretty useful knowledge for the insane circumstance we find ourselves in."

"I've studied your writings and the articles written about you," Captain Bill said. "Yes, you folks are the experts when it comes to this bizarre crap. One thing bothers me though, one big thing. From what I've read, to find your way back to the time you came from, you need to pass over the wormhole that got you there. Easier said than done. We've tried that six times so far, but we haven't hit the wormhole. We got another good celestial fix last night and aimed for what we thought was the correct position, but here we are in what goddam year I can only imagine. Instead of steaming near England, the instruments show us off Sudan on the Northwest coast of Africa. I'm not much of a drinking man, but I'm thinking of taking up the sport."

We heard a shout from the open bridge next to the captain's

office. We walked outside to see what happened. "Dear God, look at that. What the hell is that thing?" the First Officer said, pointing to starboard.

"It's a *Megalodon*," all four of US said. "A *Megalodon* is a prehistoric shark," Jenny added. "It's about 75 feet in length." From our previous time travel journeys, all four of us have become quite familiar with prehistoric wildlife, and Jenny always plugs in the particulars. Time travelers get invited to a lot of cocktail parties.

"I've always found prehistoric animals fascinating," Captain Bill said. "From my reading I know that the *Megalodon* existed over 20 million years ago. So that means that we may be 20 million years in the past." He was sweating like a beer barrel as he said that. Twenty-million years in the past?

Like I really need this shit.

Chapter 3

How's our fuel, Captain?" Jack asked. Diligent could be his middle name, and Jack always knows what questions to ask. It's one of the many reasons I love him—like crazy. He makes my self-doubt disappear. Jack's not just part of my life—he *is* my life.

"We have enough oil to steam for no more than 12,000 kilometers. Sudan is just over 10,000 kilometers from our destination in New York, so we'll need to be careful with fuel consumption, especially because I have no idea where we can refuel. I'm going to anchor in the Red Sea so we can plan our trip without running out of gas."

We dropped anchor two miles off the coast of Sudan. From photographs we have aboard, the land looked nothing like what we had in our library. We watched a herd of gigantic *Brachiosaurs* noshing on treetops. Yes, *Brachiosaurs*. According to Mike Jackson, who appointed himself as our dinosaur expert after our last experience, a *Brachiosaur* is the length of two large school buses and the height of a four-story building. Holy shit, that's bigger than the friggin House I grew up in!

Captain Bill determined that we didn't have enough food aboard because we didn't make our planned provisioning stop in England. Besides fuel, food is obviously critical. We didn't think we'd find a *Stop & Shop* in prehistoric Sudan, so it looked like a we'd need to hunt for delicacies ashore. Fortunately, like any modern ocean liner, our security crew stored plenty of ammunition, although none of it was intended for prehistoric monsters. I had a hard time wrapping my head around the idea that the captain of our luxury ship had just sent a crew ashore to hunt for food. You won't find this procedure in a Cunard Line promotional brochure.

Captain Bill dispatched a team of armed security staff—heavily armed. My *Gang* huddled on the bridge with Captain Bill as we have been doing often lately. He's a really good guy and we like working with him. Captain Bill is a former Navy man and mustered out with the rank of lieutenant commander. Jack and I felt like we knew him forever. Although Captain Bill is not that old, he reminds me of my late father.

It was scary as hell to watch as the six-man team headed toward shore on the launch. Fortunately, the sea conditions were calm. It was a large boat, which will hopefully accommodate a fresh supply of food. We watched the security guys beach the launch, tie it to a tree, and head into a forest. All of us were worried for their safety. As they traipsed through the forest, more like a jungle, they took a video, which was played on the ship via live feedback. It was as if we watched a scene of a prehistoric zoo—*Jurassic Park* on the bridge's video screen! After a few minutes we heard gunfire, and it became nonstop.

We couldn't tell whether the security guys were protecting themselves from attack by wild animals, or "shopping" for delicacies. An hour later the launch approached the ship. We could see that the aft end of the boat was loaded with carefully wrapped parcels, hopefully edible parcels. Thank God all the security guys were on the boat. None of them had become dinosaur snacks.

That evening we dined once again with Captain Bill. He enjoys having *The Wormhole Gang* around, and we like his company as well. He's a good guy and we've become seagoing pals. With trepidation, we began to eat our meal. It was a fare of different cuts of meat and some local vegetation. We were amazed that the food was quite tasty. The *QM2*'s chefs know how to use seasoning, even on prehistoric fare. The head of the shore inspection team told us that the meats were a variety of small ungulates, not dinosaurs, and it tasted a bit like lamb. So, we had one question answered—our ability to find edible food ashore. And we also have at our disposal an entire ocean of fish, some of which were 75 feet long. Bizarre shit, this time travel.

Our strange travel to a different age began to look a bit less threatening. A bit. But we still wanted to go back to where we came from, a time and place without dinosaurs, please God.

Chapter 4

The next morning, I called a breakfast meeting of *The Wormhole Gang*, Jack, Jenny, Mike, and me. We dined on a few tasty tidbits from the shore crew's findings from the day before. Although the food tasted as good as the first time I ate it, my stomach was having a hard time accepting the idea of prehistoric food. I really missed being in the present. Wouldn't you?

Before this celebration cruise, our job had been to help reverse engineer the terrorist wormhole-creating satellite, which we assumed that we accomplished. Or so we thought. I hate the phrase, *back to square one,* but that's exactly where we find ourselves—square-fucking-one, with a few million years between us and my office at the Pentagon.

Jenny put down her fork, indicating that she had something to say. When Jenny wants to talk, I'm all ears. She's smart as hell and drilled right down to the biggest issue confronting us.

"Let's face an obvious fact, guys." Jenny said. 'Unless we can find and cross the wormhole, we may as well accept the idea of becoming cave people. Finding the wormhole isn't our most important task, it's our *only* task. I have an idea."

The room went silent. When Jenny says she has an idea, your

only job is to listen. Mike put his arm around her and gave her a kiss. After the crazy stuff we've been through, I often forget that these two lovebirds are newlyweds.

"Jenny, when you say you have an idea, I speak for all of us—we're listening," I said. Jenny has a sweet, charming personality, coupled with a brain like a mainframe computer.

"Okay, so here's my thinking. From what we know about wormholes, and nobody knows more about wormholes than the four of us, there's no such thing as a wormhole that disappears. When we captured that terrorist satellite, we thought we had solved the problem, but the solution was to disable *future* wormholes from being created and had nothing to do with the existing ones. So, any wormholes that are on the earth already existed, and that presumably includes the one off Long Island that we crossed with the *QM 2*. I don't think I'm being disrespectful of the Cunard Line folks, but their helmsmen are nowhere near as talented as U.S. Navy helmsmen, most specifically my handsome honey here. Nobody is as good as Mike when manning the wheel, as we saw many times in the past. As we all know, you need to hit the coordinates of a wormhole *exactly*. Close won't do the job. Mike is the man to make that happen. I suggest that we huddle with Captain Bill and go over his paper charts and position logs. Then we need to steer directly toward the accurate coordinates we found and turn Mike loose."

Jenny's right. When not at his job as a college professor, Mike can steer a huge ship as if it was a compact car. Typical of all modern ships, the wheel isn't the large helm on older vessels, but the idea is the same—The helmsman needs to steer carefully to get where you're going.

"Jenny," I said, "you have a wonderful habit of nailing it, and I think you just did. You're absolutely right. Wormholes don't disappear, they stay where they are. Our job is to find the goddam thing and cross it. As you said, it's not our major job, it's our *only* job. I think we should huddle with Captain Bill right now."

I called Captain Bill on the bridge and he immediately picked up. I think he's beginning to see *The Wormhole Gang* as his best on-board resource. Well, it is.

"Please come up to my office, folks. I'm all ears as usual."

We told Captain Bill about our thinking that wormholes may not be where you expected to find them, especially if you're relying on electronic navigation. We showed him our ideas using the ship's chronological position log and our current chart. Sure enough, when we set down a dead reckoning position from our last celestial fix, the location of the wormhole was 20 friggin miles from where we thought we were. Obviously, the ship's electronic Dead Reckoning Tracker was malfunctioning— or had been tampered with. So, we drew a line from our last believable position and set course for the coordinates of that location. Jack and I told Captain Bill that Mike was the best helmsman we'd ever seen, and he readily agreed to let Mike take the wheel. I noticed that Captain Bill was starting to rely on us. He should. When you're traveling with experienced time travelers aboard, your number one job is to listen and pay attention. Captain Bill did just that. We estimated it would take 45 minutes to get to what we hoped was the wormhole, the longest 45 minutes of our lives. I suggested that Mike take the helm when we were 20 minutes from the target. I wanted Mike to be fully alert when we crossed the wormhole.

Fred Matthews, the First Officer, counted down the minutes to the target. At 20 minutes out, Mike took the helm.

"Thirty seconds to the wormhole, fifteen, ten…"

We felt the blessed rumbling on the deck and the daylight turned pitch dark. Yes, we found the wormhole. Jack counted down the two minutes to the other side of the wormhole. "Fifteen seconds, ten, five…We're on the target." The rumbling stopped and the darkness was replaced by bright daylight.

We did it.

But what did we do?

Chapter 5

The rumbling and light show told us we had just passed through a wormhole. But when we looked out the window on the bridge, we saw nothing but the familiar open ocean, not Long Island, the last thing we saw before we hit the wormhole. Our next task was to figure out *where* we are, not just *when* we are. Wormholes don't come with a set of instructions.

The Wormhole Gang took station on the bridge as Captain Bill had requested. He's really gotten to think a lot of us, and we think a lot of him too.

The entire crew, as well as the 2,000 passengers, had been requested to keep their eyes out for something, anything, that could tell us what year we're in. Because we had no GPS capability, we knew we weren't in the year 2021. Too bad there are no newsstands in the middle of the ocean.

"Look at the sky off the starboard side," Jenny said. We saw a gigantic flight of old fighter aircraft. There must have been over 300 of them.

"They're Grumman F6F Hellcats, the most common fighter plane in World War II." Jenny, the historian, knows her shit.

Oh my God, World War II? I was reminded of our recent time travel journey on the *Intrepid,* where we also spotted a flight of Hellcats.

We saw one of the planes drop down and circle over us.

"This is U.S. Navy Flight 239. I'm Lieutenant Gary Payton. Come in please."

He didn't address us by call sign, because obviously he had no idea who or what we were. A luxury liner like the *QM2* is not a common sight in the era of World War II, assuming that's the age we're in based on the age of the planes. Captain Bill handed the radio to me. Jenny whispered to me that the Cunard Line was founded in 1840 to give me something to say to the pilot. What we would do without Jenny I have no idea.

"Navy Flight 239 this is the *HMS Queen Mary 2*, a Cunard Line vessel," I said. "You're speaking to Ashley Patterson." I left out the "admiral" part, not wanting to freak the guy out. Let him think that I'm a civilian cruise ship officer, I figured. Although it's huge, the *QM2* is a classically designed ocean liner, so its appearance didn't look odd, unlike most modern cruise ships, which look like ocean-going resort condominiums.

I always wondered if there's a difference between an ocean liner and a cruise ship, so I asked Captain Bill. He told us that an ocean liner is a ship designed to complete a journey from one point to another, such as New York City to Southampton, England. A cruise ship, on the other hand, is designed with the onboard experience being the primary function—a floating party in other words. Ocean liners are usually better equipped than cruise ships to handle bad weather conditions and are built slightly different from cruise ships. They're big, they're beautiful, but I prefer having a good old Navy warship under me.

"My God, I've never seen such a large pleasure ship," the pilot said.

"We were recently launched. Cunard wanted to make a statement with our size." I'm learning to be a pretty good bullshitter, but I'm probably right. No doubt Cunard wanted to flex its maritime muscles to impress potential passengers and coax the credit cards from their wallets.

"Lieutenant, our ship has lost all of its navigation as well as long distance communication. Can you please tell me the accurate date including the year? Our First Officer, who is standing next to me, is under strict orders to take down the full date?" I learned this trick from Jack, a useful way to communicate strange requests. Don't just ask a stupid question, blame it on someone else.

"Today is Friday, December 4, 1941."

Holy shit, although I didn't say that. We're three days before the attack on Pearl Harbor! "Lieutenant, as I mentioned, our navigation is way off. Can you please give us an accurate position?"

He gave us our coordinates, which placed us five miles from Pearl Harbor. Oh, my God, Pearl Harbor on December 4, 1941. Last I checked, we were steaming off Long Island in the year 2021, and now we're in Hawaii just before the raid on Pearl Harbor. Have I mentioned that time travel is strange? From Long Island to Pearl Harbor in two minutes. This shit is incredible.

"If you maintain 15 knots on course 280 you should be at the entrance to Pearl Harbor in a few minutes. The call sign for the base at Pearl Harbor is *Foxtrot Xray*. I suggest that you radio them first. I doubt they will allow a civilian vessel to tie up at Pearl, but I'm sure you can get permission to drop anchor outside the base. As I guess you've heard, the Navy is on a war footing recently and is serious about security."

A war footing? I didn't mention the upcoming Japanese attack to friendly Lieutenant Payton. Why ruin the guy's day, right? We'll be talking to his superiors shortly, so he'll find out soon enough. In 1941, the Navy was edgy about Japanese intentions but knew nothing about the upcoming attack.

"This is Navy Flight 239, Lieutenant Payton signing off. Good luck with your stay at Pearl Harbor."

It was time for *The Wormhole Gang* to meet with Captain Bill and plan our frightening next few days. Our first step was to contact senior command at Pearl Harbor. I handed the radio to Jack, *Captain* Jack. No sense flipping them out by speaking to a woman admiral in 1941. Jack has an easy-going command style about him and is good at getting people to honor his requests. Always works with me. Jack got permission for us to drop anchor outside the base and for one of our shore boats to tie up at a dock near command headquarters.

Our next objective, our critical objective, was to warn the Commander of the Pacific Fleet, Admiral Husband Kimmel, that a hurricane of bad news was heading his way. Some time travel pundits say that you should never change history because you don't know what your change may bring.

Bullshit. The attack on Pearl Harbor is a piece of history that *should* be changed, and I didn't give a rat's ass what the pundits say. My *Wormhole Gang* and Captain Bill agreed. No way in hell would we not raise the red flag and warn Kimmel what would soon occur. In a strange way of looking at it, their lives were in our hands.

Good plan. But how do we communicate it to a non-time traveler?

We decided that we would simply tell the truth, including the little detail about our time travel. But first we need to get Admiral Kimmel to agree to meet with us. At my command (suggestion?) *The Gang* wore our Navy uniforms, including me with my admiral's stripes. I told the duty officer that we were on a pleasure cruise on the *QM2*. The truth, right? The guy looked at my stripes and I thought his eyes would bug out. The first female admiral would be appointed in 1972, a long way from 1941. I told the guy that my promotion to admiral was kept secret for security reasons, the only lie I told. Maybe I should write novels. I seem to have a knack for fiction, or bullshit to be more accurate. I also left out the detail of my promotion to Fleet Admiral and my appointment as Chairwoman of the Joint Chiefs of Staff. No sense in totally warping the guy's brain, right?

The clincher was when I told him that we had some critical fleet safety matters to discuss with Admiral Kimmel. The guy picked up the phone and conveyed our message to Kimmel. We were all shocked when Kimmel immediately agreed to meet us. So far so good.

We were assigned a staff car to take us to Kimmel's House. It was a huge 1938 Buick sedan with that wonderful "old car" smell.

The car took us up a long driveway to the admiral's residence. My God, what a gorgeous place, a Victorian mansion with a large sweeping lawn leading down to the water with palm trees on both sides. It had a beautiful view of Diamond Head, Hawaii's most recognized landmark. The inactive volcano got its name in the 1920s when the crew of a British ship found calcite crystals in the crater, which they thought were diamonds. They weren't, but at least they gave Diamond Head a memorable name. We were greeted at the door by a butler. A friggin butler! I totally outrank this guy Kimmel, but if it weren't for Jack's money, we'd be paupers compared to him. The Navy takes good care of its people, or at least they did in 1941. I made a mental note to put my self-doubt on hold and have a chat with my superiors. I mean, holy shit, a waterfront mansion and a butler. The 2021 Navy high command will have some explaining to do. The temperature was 81 degrees, with typically Hawaiian low humidity and a gentle breeze. It's hard not to like Hawaii.

The five of us were escorted into the house by the butler. The place was as opulent inside as the exterior. The butler led us down a long hallway to a large den.

Admiral Husband Kimmel greeted us, wearing the standard khaki uniform of the day. He introduced us to his wife, Dorothy, who was the sister of Admiral Thomas Kinkaid. "With a name like *Husband*," Kimmel said, "you wouldn't expect me to be without a wife." With that he broke out laughing.

I guessed that was his standard dumb joke when introducing his wife. Dorothy rolled her eyes.

"When you called me from base headquarters, I did some research on you folks. I understand that you said you came from another time, the year 2021, I believe, some 80 years into the future."

Jack and I had grown so accustomed to non-time traveling skeptics that we had given up trying to persuade people that we're from a different time. If they buy it, fine. If not, not. My *Gang* feels the same way.

"I hope you understand that I find this time travel story somewhat hard to believe," Kimmel said. Standard stuff.

"Yes, it is hard to believe, but it's true," I said. My usual response.

"And what comes along with that package, sir," Jack chimed in, "is that we are aware of what will happen between now and 2021. In other words, our history is *your* future."

Jack has a talent for getting people's attention. He always has mine.

"The base watch officer told me about your prediction that the Japanese will attack Pearl Harbor—on December 7 to be exact. That's three days from now. I'm going to suspend my disbelief, if only temporarily. Please tell me what you think is going to happen – according to your understanding of history."

I told Admiral Kimmel, with a lot of input from the *Gang*, exactly what happened (will happen) on December 7. I included the well-verified story of a bullet grazing Kimmel as he watched the attack, and his famous statement, "It would have been merciful had it killed me."

"A lot of people blamed you, sir," Jack said. "You'll be happy to know that in the year 2000, long after your passing, a lengthy inquiry in the United States Senate exonerated you of any malfeasance."

He seemed happy to hear that a future government let him off the hook. But I had a sinking feeling that he wasn't buying our time travel story.

"You folks have just told the watch officer that two battleships were completely destroyed, two others were sunk and recovered, one grounded, and three others badly damaged. You also told me about the other ships, including destroyers and cruisers, that were lost or damaged. So, let me ask you a simple question. In your opinion, as naval officers, why shouldn't I simply order my ships to sea the day before the attack? If your prediction of history is true, wouldn't that just save the day?"

Jenny looked at me with an expression that said she wanted to speak. I nodded my okay to her. When Jenny has a thought, I always want her to share it. As the director of the *Intrepid's* History Department, Jenny is an expert on the history of World War II, including Pearl Harbor. The *Intrepid* is one of the icons of World War II, and she took on the task of learning everything about the conflict. She has a recollection for details that I always find amazing.

"In the years after the attack," Jenny said, "a lot of people said that you should have done just that, even though you and your staff had meager information. But, sir, if you order your slower battle wagons to sea against a Japanese fleet of swift aircraft carriers, the ships would have been sunk in the deep ocean, never to have been recovered. Keeping the battleships at Pearl wasn't the big problem. Not knowing about the coming attack was the problem. I recommend, sir, and I've discussed this with Admiral Ashley and my colleagues, that you leave the battleships at Pearl. I'm sure the Japanese have spies who would alert their government that the ships left the harbor anyway.

But attached to that recommendation is this: Send as many other ships as you can muster to intercept the Japanese fleet. We have a book in the ship's library about the attack on Pearl Harbor, which includes the exact location and course of the Japanese fleet as it approached Hawaii. With an air and submarine attack, the Japanese can be stopped. We will stop them anyway, six months after the attack on Pearl Harbor, in an engagement known as the Battle of Midway, an action that will change the war in the Pacific. In that battle, we'll sink four of their carriers and one of their heavy cruisers. But what Admiral Ashley and the rest of us recommend is that we do *now,* in December 1941, what we'll do in June 1942 at the Battle of Midway. Maybe we'll even get the Japanese to a negotiating table."

Have I mentioned that Jenny knows her shit?

Kimmel looked at me.

"And what is the relationship between us and Japan in 2021, the year where you folks say you come from?"

"Good friends, strategic allies, and trading partners," I said. "The sooner we knock some sense into the heads of the militarists in Japan, the sooner we'll get to that friendly relationship."

"Admiral Patterson, Captain Thurber, I thank you for joining us this evening, along with your bright colleagues. I will take your thoughts and recommendations to my contacts in Washington."

Wonderful. Only three days before the attack on Pearl Harbor and this guy wants to confer with "his contacts" in Washington. Nothing like another meeting to put off making a decision. Meetings are the sacred ground of the procrastinator. I had the disturbing feeling that Kimmel really didn't believe us.

So, great, the Pearl Harbor attack is three days from now and this asshole's idea of decisive action is to have another meeting. The thought crossed my mind that I should convene another Senate inquiry board, and maybe reconsider this dipshit's exoneration. I shouldn't say that about him, because he seemed like a serious naval officer, but when you're a time traveler you're light on a thing called patience. The last thing you want to do is waste time.

Chapter 6

We went back to the ship, realizing that we had a big decision to make. Captain Bill had grown to rely on us. This morning he even asked me to appoint him as a member of *The Wormhole Gang*, which I happily did with the full agreement of *The Gang*. The Captain had been acting like a *Wormhole Gang*ster anyway, so why not make it official? That night we had a little party to celebrate *The Gang*'s newest member. At the party, Jenny suggested that we all stomp our feet to replicate the rumbling of a wormhole. Jack flicked the lights on and off for further realism. Maybe we should all grow up. Hell, that's no fun.

"I have the responsibility for 2,000 lives of my passengers," Captain Bill said. "No way will I leave the *Queen* anchored off Pearl. My job is to command an ocean liner, not a bomb target. Any thoughts, folks?"

"I have an idea," Jenny said. Jenny is never without ideas. She reached over to pour herself a glass of water. Before she did that, she poured ours. That's Jenny. She always puts other people first.

Mike put his arm around her and kissed her cheek.

"Don't keep us in suspense, baby. What's your idea?"

"Midway Atoll is 1,400 miles from Pearl Harbor. The United States took over Midway as a possession in 1867, and it remains a U.S. territory to this day. President Theodore Roosevelt put Midway under the command of the U.S. Navy in 1903, and the Navy constructed shore facilities. I'm sure we can refuel there, and we'll have the additional benefit of avoiding Japanese bombs. I suggest we steam for Midway immediately."

I often think that Jenny has an encyclopedia between her ears.

"Once again, Jenny, you've come up with the answer," I said. "Captain Bill, I suggest we follow Jenny's recommendation and head for Midway. Bombs are the last thing things the *QM2* needs, not to mention empty fuel tanks." Jack and Mike nodded their heads in agreement.

"I totally agree, Admiral," Captain Bill said. "We'll steam for Midway now."

We calculated it would take us 46 hours to reach Midway, which would get us there a bit over a day before the Japanese raid on Pearl Harbor. Then we'll try to figure a way to recross the wormhole back to 2021. All of this was weighing on my nerves. Jack agreed.

So, once again, we steamed for the unknown.

Chapter 7

At 0800 on December 5, we dropped anchor off Eastern Island, one of the main islands of Midway Atoll. Jenny's amazing memory told her that major shore facilities were located on that island, including a fuel depot. *The Wormhole Gang*, including its newest member, Captain Bill, boarded a shore launch and we headed for the main dock. We all wore our uniforms, including Captain Bill, sporting his Cunard Line bespoken best.

The office was manned by a Navy lieutenant, who seemed shocked to see us, to say the least, especially after looking at my stripes. Not having an intercom, he spoke into his radio.

"I've just called Commander Toliver, our base commander. I'm sure he'll want to see you folks."

Commander Dwight Toliver walked into the room. He's a tall pleasant looking man and wore his uniform as if it just came off the ironing board. He couldn't seem to take his eyes off beautiful Jenny. The lieutenant also seemed enraptured by her. Jenny grabbed Mike's hand, signaling that she's off the market. Commander Toliver then focused his stare at me. I've been told that I'm not hard to look at, and he seemed to have a hard time not looking. Following Jenny's lead, I held Jack's hand. We would later discover that no women were stationed on Eastern Island. These horny guys appeared to have a hard time adjusting to a female-free environment.

The Gang agreed that I would present *our story*. I noticed that I was developing a talent for explaining time travel to non-time travelers. Not an easy task. Just tell it like it is and let them figure it out. I went through my time travel details rather quickly, because I wanted to get to the major point—the attack on Pearl Harbor, which would begin in less than two days. They looked typically skeptical. But there in front of them were five officers, including a Fleet Admiral and the Captain of an ocean liner. Not exactly a bunch of story-telling kids.

"Admiral, and sorry but I'm having a hard time adjusting to your being a flag officer, you've just told us a story that I find unbelievable. You say that you and your ship have traveled through time, and then you said that Pearl Harbor will be attacked in less than two days. Did you bring this to the attention of Pearl Harbor command?"

"Yes, Commander, we spoke to the Commander in Chief, Pacific Fleet (CINCPACFLT)—Admiral Kimmel. Like you, he appeared to be skeptical of our story. We're worried that he didn't believe us. But here's what you need to know, Commander—It's true, every bit of it. Admiral Kimmel said that he wanted to speak to his contacts in Washington. I had the distinct feeling that he was stalling for time. But unless somebody believes our story and does something about it, over 2,400 people will be killed a couple of days from now. Also, 19 Navy ships, including eight battleships, will be damaged or destroyed. We're not bullshitting you, Commander. You need to sound the alarm."

I figured a bit of salty language might get his attention. Truth is, I felt like punching him in his time-wasting nose.

"I will contact Navy high command about this story and huddle with them."

Great, another high-level procrastinator who wants to have yet another fucking meeting.

Chapter 8

We returned to the anchored *QM2* to plan our next move. We topped off our fuel tanks from the bunkers on Eastern Island, our most important task. We paid for the oil with Cunard bank notes, and, happily, the fuel depot accepted them. Fortunately, the date wasn't pre-printed on the notes. We sat in Captain Bill's private dining room to have breakfast, although none of us were very hungry. The time was 0730 and the date was December 7, 1941. I felt nauseous. Big-brain Jenny reminded us that the first wave of the Pearl Harbor attack would begin at 0755, 25 minutes from then. We still had not received any response from Admiral Kimmel or the procrastinating shitheads at Midway. Their world was about to change, and, by not listening to us, they blew their chance to do anything about it.

Jack looked at his watch and said, "The time is 0755. *Game on!*"

Our long-range radio was working, but I almost wished that it weren't. I swallowed a grape, about the only thing my stomach could handle.

In two minutes, at 0757, the radio sounded. *"Queen Mary*

2, Queen Mary 2, this is Pearl Harbor base command, come in please."

Mike turned up the sound on the radio transmitter.

"This is Admiral Kimmel, may I please speak to Admiral Patterson?" He was out of breath, and his normally deep voice sounded like a teenage girl. The guy was obviously scared out of his mind.

"Ashley Patterson here, Admiral. We have you on speaker so we can all hear you. Please go ahead."

"I hoped I would never make this call, Admiral Ashley, but I'm afraid to tell you that your prediction was correct—*absolutely correct.* As of two minutes ago, we're under attack by Japanese dive bombers and torpedo attack planes, as I'm sure you can tell from the sounds of explosions behind me. Can you give me any details on what we can expect?"

He spoke loudly so he could be heard over the exploding sounds of war in the distance.

"Our resident historian, Jenny Blake, is next to me. She'll fill you in."

"Jenny Blake here, Admiral. I wish I had better news to give you, but here it is. The first wave of planes consisted of 183 fighters, bombers, and torpedo planes. It started its attack two minutes ago at 0755 as you well know. The second wave will consist of 170 planes and will attack at 0854, just under an hour from now. The most serious casualty will be the *USS Arizona.* One torpedo and eight bombs hit her with 1,760 lbs. of explosives as she lay moored at Ford Island Naval Station. One bomb is thought to have pierced the forward deck, setting off over one million pounds of gunpowder. 1,177 men will be killed on the *Arizona* alone. Witnesses on the *USS Nevada,* which was moored behind the *Arizona* on Battleship Row, reported that the *Arizona* sank within nine minutes. Twenty-one ships will be sunk or damaged, and 75 percent of your planes will be damaged or destroyed. Tomorrow, President Roosevelt will declare war on Japan. Because the attack was a surprise and was carried out before any pronouncement of war, Roosevelt declared December 7, 1941 as a 'Day that will live in infamy.' I'm afraid you have a terrible time ahead of you, Admiral."

I didn't think Jenny's comments made the guy feel any better, but she told it like it is. Then again, all of us had told him the same facts a few days ago, but he chose to ignore us. Bad choice, as he now realized.

Before he signed off and got back to the horrible tasks in front of him, he asked if he could contact us during the day. I agreed, of course, but there was not much we could do to help him now that the attack was on. What can an ocean liner do to help? Jack stood to speak. Jack gets attention just by standing. He gets *my* attention just by looking at me.

"According to Jenny, we know that the attack lasted two hours and was over at 0955. I suggest that we add on two hours to give the Japanese fleet time to head west and avoid encountering us. The *QM2* isn't much of a combatant, to state the obvious. Then we should head for New York and the wormhole. Captain Bill says that we have a good fix on the wormhole off Long Island, so we should head there now. Our fuel bunkers are topped off after our visit to Midway."

"I agree with Jack," I said. "Let's get the hell out of here and go back to New York and, hopefully, back to 2021." Captain Bill also agreed, as did Jenny and Mike. *The Wormhole Gang* is locked and loaded. I know that sounds very military and forceful, but my stomach was anything but locked and loaded. It was in a fucking knot.

The Long Island wormhole awaits us.

I hope.

Chapter 9

On December 14, 1941, we approached New York Harbor and the wormhole off the south shore of Long Island. We listened to a local radio station. Although the attack was seven days ago (according to the time we find ourselves in), the announcers couldn't stop giving updates about the raid on Pearl Harbor. The reports of damage and lost lives got us sick. It reminded me of the time I listened to the radio on the morning of 9/11, which many commentators likened to Pearl Harbor. And now I'm listening to reports of the attack on Pearl Harbor itself. Time travel sucks.

Jack read off the coordinates and calculated our time to reach the wormhole—15 minutes. My heart was in its usual place, my stomach. With Captain Bill's full agreement, Mike was at the helm. The time was 0935.

Jack counted down, the longest countdown we could ever imagine.

"Thirty seconds to the wormhole, ten seconds, five seconds..."

We felt the blessed rumbling as the daylight turned dark. Jack then counted down the two minutes to the other side of the wormhole. "Thirty seconds to the other side, ten seconds, five seconds..."

The rumbling stopped and the daylight returned. Off our starboard side were the beautiful mansions of the Hamptons. From the look on his face, I could tell that Jack was thinking about huddling with a real estate broker. The local radio station gave us today's date. Yes, we were back in 2021, March 4 to be exact. My God, we'd been gone a week in 1941, but in 2021 time it had been only been six hours. Have I mentioned that time travel is strange? We steamed toward the East River and our destination, Pier 12 in Brooklyn.

As we rounded the Battery, my cellphone rang. Nice to have a workable cellphone again. It was none other than Charles Atkins, aka Gamal Akhbar, but everybody knows him as Buster. He's the Director of the CIA, and probably the best it's ever had. He's a Coptic Christian, his parents hailing from Lebanon. He's well known for his ongoing war with radical Islam. "I'm a jihadi's worst nightmare," Buster would say. "I look like them and I talk like them, but I'm not one of them. I hunt them down and kill them." Unlike most CIA directors, Buster came up through the ranks as a field agent. His predecessor referred to Buster as a "super spook." Buster is well known as a man who, as he puts it, "takes no shit." Buster and I have become friends over the years.

President Blake had named Buster as the federal officer overseeing the mission to disable the terrorist wormhole-creating plot. He assigned us, along with Jenny and Mike, to his team, with me in charge. Jenny, my brilliant *Gang* member, had come up with the idea to capture the main satellite and bring it to earth so we could reverse engineer it. It was a marvelous idea, but, as we discovered on our bizarre *QM2* cruise, the plan didn't work, and the big problem is that we have no idea *why* it didn't work. Man-made wormholes are still a secret, a scary-as-hell secret. So, we still have our arms wrapped around the *Wormhole Crisis.* Or rather it has its arms around *us.*

Buster identified his location on the pier as he stood there waving at us. My heart was pounding. Maybe the CIA can figure out this shit. Captain Bill stayed behind with the *QM2* to handle the countless Cunard chores he needed to attend to.

I think Jack realized my anxiety and my constant need to feel his touch. He held my hand. Whatever life throws at me, I cannot stop loving this man, *my* man.

We piled into the CIA van and headed for Buster's New York office at 26 Federal Plaza in lower Manhattan, a bee's nest of government activity. If you're not fond of government, avoid 26 Federal Plaza.

When we walked into Buster's office, none other than Sarah Watson, Director of the FBI, awaited us. Looks like the government has pulled out all stops over the *Wormhole Crisis*. And make no doubt about it—it *is* a crisis, a bigger one than we ever imagined. Jack and I had met Sarah before on a number of occasions. In my position as Chairwoman of the Joint Chiefs of Staff, meeting with Sarah Watson was one of my regular duty requirements. Sarah is a strikingly pretty woman in her late 50s, dressed to kill, as usual, in an expensive business suit. Sarah is a classy lady.

Buster, polite as always despite his nerve-rattling job, walked around the table and poured us water. Given the scary subjects we needed to discuss, I was surprised he didn't pour himself his usual helping of scotch. He stood at the front of the room. Buster has a talent for grabbing attention. He sure as hell had ours.

"Ashley, as you and your *Gang* have recently discovered, *Operation Wormhole Kill* was a total failure," Buster said. "Jenny Blake came up with one of her typical genius ideas—to capture a wormhole-creating satellite. As great as her idea was, it didn't

39

work. And the worst part of the story is that we don't know *why* the plan didn't work. We successfully captured the goddam satellite and, using reverse engineering, we used it to destroy all the other wormhole makers in space. Finally, we disabled the damn thing. But how in hell did that wormhole suddenly appear off Long Island? It doesn't make sense. Ashley, from the look on your face I think you want to add something. Please go ahead."

"Buster, my *Wormhole Gang* has brainstormed this issue to death," I said. "The only explanation we could come up with is that the Long Island wormhole preexisted the other wormholes. It was there all along. The satellite we captured was only intended to create future wormholes."

"But here's the problem with that scenario, Ashley. The Long Island wormhole is located smack in the middle of one of the busiest shipping lanes in the country, if not the world—the entrance to New York Harbor. Through the Coast Guard, we've sent out a steady stream of *Notice to Mariners* to prevent other ships from crossing the thing, as the *QM2* did. Two days ago, we received a report that a large pleasure yacht went missing. Could it have sunk? Possibly, but constant searches have not shown any wreckage, so we're operating on the theory that the yacht is lost somewhere in time. So, we're back to where we started, hostages to terrorist wormhole-creating satellites. Our country is on the verge of being torn apart. Sarah, your comments?"

Sarah Watson's photo should appear in Wikipedia next to the words, "Sharp Cookie." She doesn't miss a thing, and that includes the mystery of the secret wormhole. She stood to speak.

"This crisis requires action, decisive action. Sitting around and talking about it won't accomplish anything. Something tells me that we'll find the answer, if there is an answer, on the other side of the wormhole. Ashley, I wouldn't say this without your full agreement, but I'm clear that you should take command of a warship, or better yet a Carrier Strike Group, and move this operation forward. With your okay I will contact the White House and the Office of Naval Operations."

I looked at Jack, who simply smiled and nodded his head. Our habit of communicating with just a nod or glance was on full display.

Jenny and Mike also looked at me. "We're in, Admiral Ashley," Jenny said, as Mike vigorously nodded his head.

———————

We were about to leave Buster's office when Sarah Watson called for attention.

"Man-made time travel isn't the only crisis we're facing," Sarah said. "A horrible virus has just been turned loose on the world." Buster's assistant quickly walked into the office. "Buster, I recommend that we look at a major announcement on the TV."

"Dana Perino here for *Fox News* and the *Daily Briefing*, ladies and gentlemen. In the past few days, we've been hearing disturbing reports of a fast-spreading deadly virus that originated in Wuhan, China. The virus is known as *COVID-19*, a *Coronavirus*. Just this morning, the World Health Organization, labeled the contagion a *pandemic*, which is a world-wide epidemic. The President has declared a National Emergency, unlocking billions of federal funds to fight the problem. The Centers for Disease Control (CDC) in Atlanta announced that fighting the COVID-19 pandemic is at the top of its list of priorities.

"The CDC has issued a set of rules, which so far are voluntary. The rules include the wearing of face masks when in public and maintaining a 'social distance' of six feet from another person. The CDC also recommends that you stay home unless it's absolutely necessary to venture forth. Some states have taken the economically drastic step of shutting down businesses, and hence the state economies. If you're in the restaurant business, chances are you're out of business.

"Following up on the President's executive actions, the Senate has passed the *Coronavirus Aid, Relief, and Economic Security Act* (CARES), providing $2 trillion in aid to hospitals, small businesses, and state and local governments.

"According to the CDC, this is the worst public health crisis since the 1918 Flu Pandemic with the H1N1 virus. I recommend that anyone watching this show follow the CDC safety recommendations.

"This announcement comes on the heels of the bizarre *Man-Made Time Travel Crisis,* also known as the *Wormhole Crisis,* named for the locations on earth where people can literally travel, unintentionally, from one time to another.

"Stay tuned for updates on these horrifying crises that our nation, indeed the world, faces. Dana Perino signing off for *Fox News.*"

Buster's assistant turned off the TV.

"Admiral Ashley, you, Jack, and your *Gang* are front and center in confronting this *Wormhole Crisis,*" Buster said. "Keep in touch and let my office know of anything new you encounter. My aide, Micky, will now give each of you a face mask. Wear them well and wear them often, especially when indoors."

The Wormhole Gang was about to weigh anchor, keeping six

feet from one another and wearing our face masks.

This shit is beyond weird.

Chapter 10

Vice Admiral John (Jake) Wayman, Chief of Naval Operations, asked me to visit him in his office in the Pentagon, a floor below mine. I walked into his office and sat six feet from him. We would normally shake hands after saluting, but given the rules of COVID-19, we settled for just a salute. I removed my face mask because we were sitting. As a newly minted Fleet Admiral and Chairwoman of the Joint Chiefs of Staff, I technically outrank him, even though he's CNO, so he "asked" me to his office, not "ordered." I've known Jake for a few years, and think of him as a good guy, not one given to bullshit, which is high on my list of priorities.

"Ashley, because you vastly outrank me, I won't give you any orders, I'll simply relay orders from the White House. President Blake wants you to assume command of Carrier Strike Group 3400. The *USS Gerald R. Ford* will be your flagship. The other four ships making up the group are all frigates, the *USS Bronstein*, the *Garcia*, the *Knox*, and the *Oliver Hazard Perry*. I know that you like to have your *Wormhole Gang* with you, and I've gotten them approved to report aboard. Your assignment is simple but carrying it out won't be. The President wants you to succeed where *Operation Wormhole Kill* failed, to put a final end to those goddam satellite-created wormholes. Although I really don't understand this time travel stuff beyond what I've learned from you and Jack, I assume that you will want to conduct your activities on the other side of a wormhole, presumably the one off the south shore of Long Island.

So, there are your orders, Ashley. Although you're the highest-ranking officer in the Navy, you will have a seagoing command under you. I don't envy the tough job that you're facing, but I'm confident as hell that President Blake chose the best officer possible, which, of course, is you. You will relieve Admiral Miles Franken, and he's expecting your visit. You're scheduled to take command the day after tomorrow. Best of luck, my friend. We'll be talking again soon. Please give my best regards to Jack."

Wow, I'll command a Carrier Strike Group. I didn't know whether to be excited, flattered, or scared shitless. I opted for scared shitless.

Jack was with me in Washington that day.

"Jack, honey, I hope Thurber Publishing can do without you for a while. I've just been given command of a Carrier Strike Group with the *USS Gerald R. Ford* as my flagship. Looks like Naval Operations and the President agree with Sarah Watson. My job is to complete the efforts of *Operation Wormhole Kill.* Please say that you can join me as my Chief of Staff. Jenny and Mike will be with us, as usual. Given the new COVID-19 rules, this assignment will be somewhat strange, but, like all of us, I follow orders. Please say yes, baby."

The idea of taking on this job without Jack at my side simply didn't clear muster with my brain. I don't just love him, I *need* him.

"One of the best things I've done with Thurber Publishing was to hire talented executives," Jack said. "The company will do fine without me. No way in hell will I be without you, honey. When do we go?"

"The day after tomorrow. Can you join me this afternoon to meet the guy I'm succeeding, Admiral Miles Franken? Also at the meeting will be Captain Luke Barrett, CO of the *Ford.* We'll take a flight to Norfolk, where the group is docked."

"As your Chief of Staff, your husband, and your lover, how can I possibly say no, baby? I'll meet you at the Pentagon in a half-hour."

So, I've just been given the scariest command of my life. At least I'll have my *Wormhole Gang* with me, including Jack, the most important person in my life. Having the right people with you makes the toughest command easier. Not easy, just a bit easier.

So, back to wormhole hunting. And now we have to worry about 'social distancing' and face mask wearing. Have I mentioned that this shit is getting old?

Chapter 11

Jack and I met with Admiral Miles Franken, the guy I'll succeed as Commanding Officer of Carrier Strike Group 3400. I've known Miles for a few years and admire his strict take-no-prisoners attitude. He graduated from Annapolis three years before me and we've known each other since then. As tough as he is, I think Franken felt relieved that I was taking over his command, one with a frightening new mission.

Jack and I stayed overnight at one of the numerous apartments at Naval Station Norfolk. Over the years I had been stationed at Norfolk many times, so we felt at home. It wasn't the luxury accommodation that Jack likes, but hell, we have our orders and we're on assignment. We had dinner at the Officer's Club with Captain Luke Barrett, the Commanding Officer of the *Ford*, a guy who I'll work closely with. Barrett had already been briefed about the scary wormhole-hunting mission of CSG 3400. In accord with COVID-19 rules, we removed our face masks only because we were seated.

"Admiral, serving under you and Captain Jack is the highlight of my career. I won't let you down."

His role as CO of the flagship was an important one, and

I was happy to see that he was ready for it. Having the right people around you helps get the job done. That's almost a cliché but it's true. The right people are critical, and Captain Barrett and my *Wormhole Gang* are *the right people.*

The next morning Jack and I will move our belongings into "Admiral's Country" on the *Ford*, the odd name for the quarters where we'll hang out.

As we climbed the gangway, we heard the officer of the deck announce, "Carrier Strike Group 3400, arriving," the Navy's time-honored way of announcing a dignitary, along with the person's title. I guess I've arrived. As my Chief of Staff, Jack wore a fancy shoulder ribbon which identified his assignment. I told him he looked sexy as hell, resulting in a kiss and a pinch to my ass. We may be hot shit Navy brass, but bottom line, it's just me and Jack.

Jenny and Mike came aboard half an hour later. *The Wormhole Gang* had lunch in my fancy new digs. They both carried the title as my aides. Between bites, Jenny would reach over and squeeze Mike's hand. I was happy to see that they still acted like newlyweds. Jenny, no surprise, had already prepared a draft of my first address to all hands of CSG 3400. As an original member of *The Wormhole Gang*, Jenny put in all the details, allowing for security of course, about our mission—which is to put a final end to wormhole creating and give truth to the title of the mission, *Operation Wormhole Kill.* Just how the hell we would do that is a thought that was constantly on my mind, and on the minds of *The Gang.* Maybe we'll just drift around in the ocean, hold an inter-ship video Scrabble tournament, and see what happens. I hate not having a plan, but planning for the unknown is a talent I have yet to acquire.

On Friday morning CSG 3400 was scheduled to depart for the wormhole off Long Island. At 0900, the officer of the deck of the *Ford* announced through the loudspeakers of all five ships of CSG 3400:

"Attention all hands, Attention all hands. Stand by for the Commanding Officer of Carrier Strike Group 3400, Admiral Ashley Patterson."

"Good morning, everyone," I said. "Today we will do something that is seldom accomplished. We will intentionally cross a wormhole and travel back in time. Some of you have done this before, but all of you have been briefed. When our ship crosses the wormhole, you will feel rumbling under your feet and the sky will turn pitch dark. After exactly two minutes, the rumbling will stop, and the daylight will return, indicating that we've traveled through time. Our mission is critical to our nation's security, and I will keep you briefed during our journey. We've been ordered to carry out the most important operation imaginable. I look forward to seeing you all in the past. That is all. Carry on."

Jack was standing next to me when I made the announcement.

"Don't ask me why, but I get all horny when you announce, 'carry on.' You have a sexy way of ending an announcement."

"Hey, handsome, tonight I'll show you exactly how I intend to 'carry on.' And don't even think about social distancing. You game?"

"I'm more than game, baby. How about a warmup kiss?"

Jack and I have a way of communicating that you will not find in Naval Regulations.

At 1500 hours the five ships of Carrier Strike Group 3400 approached the coordinates of the wormhole off Eastern Long

Island, with the *Ford* in the lead. We had practiced this exacting maneuver countless times. The *Ford*, with Mike Jackson at the helm, successfully made it through the wormhole. I looked out the window and, sure enough, the mansions of the Hamptons had disappeared. We were in a different time. The *Ford* was followed by the *USS Bronstein*, the *Garcia*, the *Knox*, and the *Oliver Hazard Perry*. Every one of them successfully made it through the wormhole on the first attempt. God bless our helmsmen! I made a mental note to host a party for these guys the next time we're in port.

Our COVID-19 rules, with face mask wearing and social distancing, were turning out to be nothing more than a pain in the ass, an inconvenience. But faced with the prospect of contracting a dangerous virus, we all put up with the pain in the ass. Being inconvenienced beats the hell out of dying from a virus.

I decided to follow the exact course we took the last time we went through this wormhole. I didn't have a certain reason why, but it seemed to be a good idea to retrace our steps.

So, two weeks after we crossed the wormhole, CSG 3400 steamed near Sudan off the northwest coast of Africa.

We looked toward shore through binoculars. We didn't see any dinosaurs, thank God. So, we made it through the wormhole. Now what? The *Wormhole Crisis* is still a secret, and the crisis is still a crisis. And the pandemic is still the pandemic.

Chapter 12

Jack and I stood next to each other on the bridge as CSG 3400 steamed south of Sudan. Because we were obscured by a bulkhead, we held hands, as usual. I cannot possibly live without this man's touch. Have I mentioned how much I love Jack?

"Looks like we have company," Jack said as he pointed off our starboard bow. A beautiful four-masted brig gracefully made her way through the sea. From my reading I knew that a brig is typically between 75 and 165 feet in length. The ship we observed was every bit of 150 feet, making it one of the larger ones ever launched. It looked like floating history. In my office on the *Ford* I have a painting of a brig that appeared exactly like the ship we looked at. Her sails were filled with wind and she heeled slightly to port. From her flags, we could see that the ship was part of the British Royal Navy. The name painted on her hull identified the ship as *HMS Endeavor*.

Jenny joined us on the bridge with a thick book from the ship's library tucked under her arm. It was a book that identified ships of the Royal Navy from 1800 to the present. Jenny doesn't like surprises, and always prepares for them.

"*The Endeavor* was active at sea from 1830 to 1875," Jenny

said. "Obviously, the ship has no radio, so if we want to hail her, we'll need to do so by loudspeaker. I doubt that they can read semaphore signals."

I turned to Jack. "Let's make it happen, baby. Tell them we want to visit."

Jack picked up the microphone.

"My name is Captain Jack Thurber, Executive Officer of the *USS Gerald R. Ford,* a ship of the United States Navy. With your permission, we would like to send a launch to you and come aboard." Actually, Jack is the Executive Officer of Carrier Strike Group 3400, but we figured that our 19th Century British friends had no idea what a Carrier Strike Group is, so why confuse them. We were about 300 feet from the *Endeavor.*

A man wearing the historic uniform of a British naval officer, stood on the open bridge holding what looked like a megaphone. Jenny told us that back then it was known as a "speaking trumpet." Leave it to Jenny to come up with fascinating details. Holy shit, a *speaking trumpet?*

"We welcome you aboard," the man shouted into his megaphone/speaking trumpet. "Please tie your boat to the base of the ladder amidships on our port side."

The *Endeavor* pointed into the wind and dropped sails so we could climb aboard.

Jack, Jenny, Mike, and I, *The Wormhole Gang,* boarded the shore launch, the oddly named the "Admiral's Barge," and headed for the *Endeavor.* We were helped aboard by three polite British sailors. At the top of the ladder, we were greeted by a man named Nigel Kingsmith, the Captain of the ship. His 19th century uniform could best be described as charming. He wore white knee-length socks below his trousers, and his form-fitting jacket was adorned with ribbons. Both sides of his hat were peaked toward the top. Hanging from his belt was a two-foot cutlass. From the look on his face, I couldn't tell, as the old saying goes, whether he needed to shit or go blind. Being boarded by a group of oddly dressed officers from the most gigantic ship he had ever seen was not on his list of things to do that day.

I explained, awkwardly, the COVID-19 pandemic problem and handed them face masks. Although we found ourselves in a different era of time, I realized that we could all be carrying the transmittable virus. Easy going guys, they didn't seem to mind wearing the face masks.

He and his First Lieutenant, Jeremy Campbell, escorted us to the captain's office, just behind the bridge. A First Lieutenant was the rank back then for the second in command, now known as the Executive Officer. Along the port and starboard bulkheads in the cabin were portholes, not windows. Unlike a modern ship, the bulkheads weren't gray, but beautifully polished wood. We could hear the beams creak as the ship gently rocked in the ocean. Beautiful is the only way I can describe the ship. I felt like I was watching an old movie. First Lieutenant Campbell uncorked a large bottle of Scotch whiskey. These guys know how to welcome guests. Because we were all sitting—six feet apart—we removed our face masks.

Jack introduced us, including me, an admiral from the 21st Century. I don't know if people freaked out in the 1800s, but that's exactly what they appeared to do. A woman admiral? They'll get used to it. Everybody does. I then embarked on my essential task, my fun task—to explain who we are and what we're doing at sea with five strange-looking ships, one of which, my flagship the *USS Gerald R. Ford*, was gigantic beyond their wildest imaginations.

Captain Nigel couldn't have been more gracious as he poured himself a healthy helping of scotch. Wanting my mind as clear as possible, I refused his offer of booze. The rest of the *Gang* declined as well. When time traveling, it's difficult to tell if you're drunk or sober, so why make it any more complicated? I tried, with my time traveler best, to explain just what it means to travel through time. They looked stunned. Who could blame them?

The most fun part of my presentation was the *Ford* itself. I explained that the *Ford* was 1,206 feet in length and weighed over 100,000 tons. What really got interesting was my description of her propulsion—nuclear power, which gave her a cruising range of at least 45 years, probably more. Our British friends were silent, dead silent. They both poured themselves more scotch, a lot more. Besides her size, range, and nuclear power, these two couldn't wrap their heads around the idea that the *Ford,* known as an aircraft carrier, actually launches and recovers bizarre machines called airplanes, machines that fly in the air like birds.

"So, if I understand you, Admiral, your mission is to put an end to these wormhole things that you just told us about, especially man-made wormholes. Your description of everything takes my breath away, especially those amazing flying machines you call aircraft. May I remind you, we are in the year 1850, 170 years from the time you say you came from. Dear Lord, what advances mankind has made over those years."

"So, Captain, from what you've said, none of your people have experienced this strange phenomenon of time travel."

"My mind is reeling, Admiral. From your stories, I'm beginning to think that England just may have experienced time travel. Over the years, a number of our ships have gone missing without leaving any debris, and their whereabouts are unknown. You've got me thinking that maybe those ships encountered those things you call wormholes and disappeared to another era of time."

Captain Nigel amazed me with his open-mindedness, which took some doing for a 19th Century guy listening to stories about the 21st Century.

I then explained just what a Carrier Strike Group is, and that I'm the Commanding Officer of CSG 3400. Yes, a female admiral. Captain Nigel and his First Lieutenant poured themselves another large helping of scotch.

"From what you folks told us, England and America are close allies in the year you come from. Therefore, I pledge the *Endeavour* to your aid. We'll do whatever we can to help you with your strange mission. Consider the *Endeavor* part of your Carrier Strike Group thing, even though we will not be able to match your speed—or help you to fly those strange airplane machines."

Although I had no idea what the *Endeavour* could do for us, it just seemed like a good idea to have help from a ship in local time. Captain Nigel seemed like a hell of a nice guy and a serious commanding officer. Jack handed them two long-range radios with extra batteries. If we're going to have their help, we need to communicate with them. Jack showed them the simple steps in using a wireless radio. They looked like a couple of kids under a Christmas tree as they tested their new radios.

Captain Nigel told us they were going to anchor off Sudan to perform some routine maintenance. We said goodbye, a temporary goodbye, to our new pals from the past.

Chapter 13

Before we left New York, we met with Rear Admiral Michael Dunton, the new Director of the Department of Defense Science Department. According to Dunton, DOD had made huge inroads with the top secret "wormhole detector," a device that can pick up electromagnetic pulses emitted by a wormhole, thereby helping to locate and identify it. When we first met with DOD a few months before, we were told that they had invented a rudimentary device that could detect a wormhole, but you needed to be right on top of the thing and point the device directly at it. Now, with the huge recent advances in technology, the device can pick up faint signals from a wormhole as far away as three miles. The closer you get, the louder the return signal. Each detector came with a dozen small "repeaters" which you can hook onto your belt. Beside the sound, the devices also show the coordinates of the wormhole and the course to get to it. After we drop anchor, I planned to distribute the repeaters to a select group of people including, of course, my *Wormhole Gang*.

My God, what a breakthrough. Before now, the only way to detect a wormhole was to cross the damn thing. I will order each of the ships of Carrier Strike Group 3400 to be equipped with the detector and the repeaters, which I'll distribute when we all meet. But I didn't announce it yet. I wanted to make sure the device worked before I shared it with the captains in my group. Hopefully, the instrument will eliminate the worst aspect of a wormhole—surprise. *The Wormhole Gang* put our heads together and came up with a name for the wormhole detection device—a *Wormy*.

Jack and I had just finished our morning run around the flight deck. It was hot at 85 degrees, but the humidity wasn't bad. After our run we continued to walk around the deck having one of our impromptu meetings as we often do. Meeting or not, I just love being with Jack. However my day is going, when I'm with Jack it goes better. I don't know whatever I did to deserve a man like him, but I want to keep doing it. Jack makes our strange circumstances tolerable, even fun. Jack's the man—*my man*.

As we turned near the forward end of the flight deck and headed aft, we heard a faint sound from our *Wormies.* Oh my God, we've detected another wormhole. I hoped the thing worked as claimed. We immediately went to the flag bridge to communicate to the other ships in CSG 3400. All the COs of the other ships knew what we were about to do—cross the wormhole and figure it out from there, although they didn't yet know about the *Wormy.* I radioed Captain Nigel on the *Endeavor* to let him know that we're about to cross a wormhole. Although I would love to have the *Endeavor* with us, no way can it match our speed, which is 30 knots at full throttle. Top speed for the *Endeavor* is seven knots, provided there's a stiff wind.

As we approached the target coordinates, the five ships of CSG 3400 lined up, with the *Ford* in the lead. None of the captains were aware of our wormhole detecting devices—yet. I looked forward to breaking the *Wormy* news to them. We headed into a light wind, which was a good thing to keep us on an exact course. Jenny and Mike, the rest of the *Wormhole Gang*, stood with Jack and me as we headed for the target. I was surprised and happy to see the *Endeavor* a few hundred feet off to starboard. Captain Nigel called me on the radio—He *loves* his new radio— and said they would give it an attempt to join us through the wormhole, sailing behind the *USS Knox*, the last ship in our group. Heading into the light wind, the *Endeavor* was even slower than usual. Although the ship was no speed demon, she had a crew of experienced ocean sailors, skilled mariners who make the rest of us look like amateur weekend boaters. Sailing under wind power is a lot more challenging than steaming with a nuclear reactor. Also, Captain Nigel now had a modern gyrocompass that Jack had given him. I ordered the group speed to be 10 knots so as not to leave *Endeavor* too far behind.

Jack held up the *Wormy* and got the signal we were looking for.

We felt the rumbling beneath us as the daylight turned dark. All five ships of CSG 3400 made it through the wormhole. I ordered all ships to cut their engines so we could go adrift and hopefully spot the *Endeavor.* Jenny, no surprise, had calculated the time for *Endeavor* to cross the wormhole, based on the ship's estimated speed. She raised her right hand and then brought it down quickly. She pointed toward the site.

"Now!" Jenny yelled. There, in her square-rigged beauty, was the *Endeavor.* Every person on every ship in the group who saw her shouted and clapped their hands. I called Captain Nigel on his new radio.

"Nigel, my friend, if you tag along with us to the 21st Century, I'm sure I can convince the American Navy to put you in command of a U.S. Navy warship. You did a fabulous job of seamanship when you crossed the wormhole. I see that we're in somewhat shallow water, so I'm about to order all ships in the group to drop anchor. We'll then have a command meeting here on the *Ford*. As one of the proud captains of Carrier Strike Group 3400, you're invited, of course. I'll send a launch to pick you up."

I felt like I just made Captain Nigel's day, if not his year. Maybe his career?

The next part of the plan is, well, that's what the meeting is about.

Chapter 14

T he captains of CSG 3400 boarded the *Ford* and sat around the large table in the conference room next to the wardroom. My *Wormhole Gang* was there, of course. Jenny, finding it impossible to control her innate kindness, took on the chore as hostess of the meeting. Wearing her face mask, she walked around the table with snacks and iced tea for everybody.

Jack entered the room with Captain Nigel Kingsmith and Commander Jeremy Campbell, our special guests and newest members of CSG 3400. I introduced them and everyone in the room stood and applauded our British friends from the past.

Nigel and Jeremy looked like they had just been awarded the Victoria Cross.

"It's my honor to welcome Captain Nigel Kingsmith and his second in command, First Lieutenant Jeremy Campbell of the *HMS Endeavor.* Although he's in the British Royal Navy, Captain Nigel has volunteered to assist us in the mission of CSG 3400 and I'm happy to have him aboard. This is his first time aboard a nuclear warship. As skipper of a square rigger, he showed us all a thing or two about seamanship as he navigated his ship through the wormhole."

Everybody politely applauded.

Nigel and Jeremy sat there, beaming.

"Before I babble on any further, I want to know if any of you folks have questions." Commander Elizabeth Parker, Commanding Officer of the *USS Oliver Hazard Perry*, raised her hand. "Go ahead, Betty."

She stood and saluted me.

"Admiral Ashley, I first want to say what an honor it is to serve under you, the best friggin admiral in the United States Navy, in my humble opinion." The room broke out in applause. Betty Parker and I have been friends for years, and I always enjoy her sweet sense of politeness.

"My question is this, Admiral. How can we solve a problem if we don't really know what the problem is? Sure, we know that man-made time travel is the problem, but where do we start without finishing up like the ill-named *Operation Wormhole Kill?* I mean, shit, pardon my French, but do we even know what we're looking for?"

"Yes, Betty, I pardon your French, because that's where we find ourselves—up to our eyeballs in shit. I wish I could provide an answer, but here's the best I can come up with. We don't have a simple objective, as much as we'd like one. We're all senior naval officers, but our jobs are more like that of gumshoe detectives. We need to look for clues, and we'll know that we've found something when it happens. The biggest breakthrough we've had in this mess is the wormhole detecting device and the little repeaters that we just distributed to you folks. Jack will give you a brief seminar on how to use the devices, which is quite simple. My *Wormhole Gang* has come up with a memorable name for the instrument—a *Wormy*. Before this breakthrough, the only way you know you've encountered a wormhole is when you crash into the thing. Now at least we'll see it before we hit it. For now, at least, we know navigation logs must be kept with the greatest precision and always up to the minute.

"We already know a few things about our mission before we even begin. We know, from the conclusion of the Department of Defense, that a wormhole can be created on earth by a satellite in space. We know what it feels like when you've hit the thing, the rumbling, the sudden darkness, and the passage of two minutes to the other side of the wormhole. We also know that to go back to where you came from, you have to pass exactly through the same spot, precisely. So, we know the answer we're looking for—to prevent wormholes from happening. But we don't know how to get to that answer."

Commander Brad Fletcher, CO of the *USS Knox*, raised his hand.

"Yes, Brad."

"Admiral, I constantly hear mention of the *Wormhole Gang*. Can you tell us who or what they are?"

"It's a name I gave to a group of four, count 'em four, people who were involved in the dramatic time travel event when I was the temporary Commanding Officer of the museum aircraft carrier, the *USS Intrepid,* a story you have all heard. All four *Wormhole Gang* members are in this room. You all know my husband, Captain Jack, the original Gang member. Lt. Commander Jenny Blake, the lovely lady who just served us snacks, is also a charter member, as is her husband, Mike Jackson. I'm happy to say that I joined them in marriage in a wonderful at-sea ceremony while on the *Intrepid.* Jenny and Mike are senior volunteers with the *Intrepid* museum. In their civilian lives they were both professors at Columbia University. They are now on active duty with the Navy, both as lieutenant commanders, a promotion given them by none other than President Blake, who is Jenny's close cousin. So that, including me, is the *Wormhole Gang.*"

"Admiral Ashley, if I may?"

"Go ahead Betty."

"I recommend, Admiral, actually I request, that you deputize all of us as members of the *Wormhole Gang.* Together, under your leadership, we'll find the solution to the *Wormhole Crisis.*"

Everybody in the room stood and applauded Commander Betty's request. Jenny, no surprise, walked around the room and pinned a lovely red ribbon on each captain's chest. Among her many hobbies, Jenny loves to create decorative ribbons.

"I proudly decorate you folks with my latest invention, the *Wormribbon.*" From the smiles on their faces, everybody seemed to get a big kick out of their latest decoration.

Captain Nigel of the *Endeavor* raised his hand.

"Please don't forget me, mum," he said to Jenny, "Nothing can make me prouder than to be a *Wormhole Gang* member."

She did just that, saluted him, and, wearing her face mask, gave him a hug.

Our meeting came to an end. We all realized that we had one big piece of unfinished business.

Where, and when, are we?

Chapter 15

Carrier Strike Group 3400 got underway, but we had no idea where we were, in time or in place. God, do I ever miss satellite navigation. Jenny showed Captain Nigel and Commander Jeremy to their stateroom. Captain Nigel had decided to leave the *Endeavor* at anchor with a lieutenant in command. Jack gave another radio to Captain Nigel, who then gave it to the lieutenant. Nigel was committed to helping *The Gang* with its mission in any way he could. Jenny also took them to the ship's store so they could find U.S. Navy uniforms, more in keeping with their new status as *Wormhole Gang* members as well as officers of Carrier Strike Group 3400. Jenny also gave them extra face masks.

As usual, I huddled with the *Gang*, my original *Gang*, Jack, Jenny, Mike, and me. Mike, who always wears binoculars hanging from his neck, spotted land on the horizon. I decided to head there. Why not? Jack alerted the captains of the other ships of our intention. Jack had quickly become the liaison between the command of CSG 3400 (me) and the other ships in the group. I can do without Jack as easily as I can do without air.

The captains of CSG 3400 acknowledged the order. We steamed toward the land, having no idea what we'd find.

We were in for a shock.

Chapter 16

Nigel and Jeremy entered the bridge, wearing their U.S. Navy uniforms that Jenny had procured from the ship's store. They looked great, but somehow, I missed their 19th Century duds.

The land we came upon was a large island. We were a half mile from shore in 150 feet of water. I ordered all ships to drop anchor to give us the opportunity to observe what's around us. I was shocked to see a large number of small buildings. Not a dinosaur in sight, thank God. We couldn't determine anything from the ship, so I dispatched a platoon of 20 SEALs to go ashore in a launch, led by Lieutenant Miles Ferguson. Each SEAL was heavily armed because we had no idea what kind of wildlife, animal or human, that they may encounter. The buildings told us that we were far from a prehistoric past, but we didn't know if the buildings housed friendly people.

The launch returned and Lt. Ferguson reported to the flag bridge where Jack and I were meeting with Jenny and Mike. With him were two men dressed in expensive tasteful clothing, each wearing khaki slacks, a Navy-blue blazer, and Ferragamo loafers. They looked like a Brooks Brothers ad. Ferguson had already explained to them our COVID-19 virus problem, and they both wore face masks. He introduced them as Bill Wellfleet and Peter Hall, Bill's assistant. They spoke perfect English I was happy to hear. They even had American accents and used modern American colloquialisms, such as "Wazzup, bro." Bill said they were with an organization known as *The Keepers of Time*, whatever the hell that is. We'd soon find out. I asked him what year we're in. He didn't seem at all put off by my telling him that we had time traveled. From our conversation I could tell that they were quite familiar with the phenomenon. They told us to call them by their first names. Pleasant guys.

"You are in the year 2230, Admiral. Welcome to the future."

Holy shit, we've time traveled *forward* over 200 years! I pulled up a stool and sat, to avoid falling over.

"Bill, can you tell us where we are?"

"In the time you came from, Admiral, that land off our starboard side was known as Long Island, a part of what was then New York State, which was part of a land then known as the United States of America. Now it is called, simply, *The Island.*"

Jack sensed that I wanted to communicate with the CSG 3400 captains. I never need to tell Jack what's on my mind. He knows me—better than I do.

"Attention all hands, attention all hands, stand by for the Commanding Officer of Carrier Strike Group 3400, Admiral Ashley Patterson," Jack announced.

He pinched me on my ass, his usual way of letting me know it's time to speak. He's always discrete enough to make sure nobody is watching. Jack is cool. He's also quite hot, as he reminded me last night.

"Good afternoon everyone. As you all know by now, we have once again traveled to another era, this time to the future, 209 years into the future to be exact. I'll pause for a moment to give you time to appreciate what I've just said. Yes, we're 209 years into the future. According to the two gentleman who have come aboard, that land off to starboard was once Long Island, and is now known as *The Island*. As of now, we're no closer to our objective than we were before. But our objective still remains clear, if somewhat muddled, on how to get there. I will keep you all up to date as we learn more. Please come to the *Ford* and climb aboard. I want to hold a lunch meeting of the expanded *Wormhole Gang* and our visitors from the future."

Sometimes I get fed up with meetings, but I couldn't wait for this one to start. It isn't every day that you get to meet with people from over 200 years into the future.

Captain Kingsmith and Jeremy Campbell were still with us from the *Endeavor*. When we first met, we were 170 years in the past. Now we're over 200 years into the future. They looked confused, even with their face masks.

At 1300 all the captains filed into the large conference room in Admiral's Country on the *Ford*. I introduced Bill Wellfleet and Peter Hall. They both seemed relaxed, not at all intimidated by being asked to speak to a large crowd.

"Bill, I understand that you are the leader of your organization. Please tell us your title and what your group is all about."

Bill stood in the front of the room and removed his face mask to speak. This guy seemed comfortable in a leadership position.

"My name is Bill Wellfleet, and my title is *The Samah*. Some people think my title is some lofty word from an ancient language. Truth is, the title was first bestowed on my distant great grandfather, Ezekiel Wellfleet, the founder of our organization, over 200 years ago. He was hosting a group of his advisors when someone suggested that Grandpa Zeke should have a title. Grandpa walked over to a window and saw a maintenance truck parked outside. Written on the sides of the vehicle were the words, *Samah Plumbing and Heating.* So, their exalted ruler acquired a title, *The Samah.* "

Everybody cracked up at the funny story. Easy to like these guys.

"Which brings us to the next question, Bill. What, pray tell, is *The Keepers of Time?*"

"It's an organization that was founded two years after the beginning of *The Great War Crisis,* which started on April 13, 2022, the date the world ended."

The room became so silent you could hear a bird feather crash onto the deck. Bill had our total attention. Oh my God, the end of the world?

"That's a bit less than a year from now, now being the time we came from, the year 2021." My heart was pounding like a drum.

"A newspaper headline from the day before the war says it all," Bill said. "I've memorized it:

Nuclear Talks between Iran and the United States Falter as Large Amounts of Iranian Weapons Delivered to North Korea - President Puts Military on High Alert

"The next day saw the beginning of a worldwide nuclear war," Bill continued. "From where you folks come, it hasn't happened—*yet.* But make no mistake, it's on its way. How would you like a tour of New York City, more than 200 years after it was destroyed?"

In a room full of senior military officers, there was only one answer to his question—yes. We need to see New York City— and what happened to it, or more to the point, what *will happen* to it. It's our job to know what's going on and try to figure out a way to do something about it. That will be the tricky part. The other captains returned to their ships. On my command, we weighed anchor and began the most upsetting journey any of us would ever take, especially me. I was born and raised in New York City, Whitestone, Queens to be exact. I wasn't even close to being ready for the horror we were about to see.

Carrier Strike Group 3400 steamed for New York Harbor. As we approached Staten Island, we came upon a stomach-turning sight. Two tall towers appeared before us, one on each side of the waterway. A single cable stretched from one tower to the other, from what was once Fort Hamilton on the Brooklyn side to Fort Wadsworth on Staten Island. They were no longer identifiable as military installations, just mounds of debris. From the cable hung dozens of smaller cables, swinging gently in the light breeze. We were looking at the over 200-year-old remains of the Verrazano-Narrows Bridge. All of the ships in the group paid close attention to our omnidirectional sonar so as to avoid hitting any submerged debris. I felt nauseous. I recalled my parents telling me all about how they watched the lovely Verrazano-Narrows Bridge being built. It opened in 1964, 17 years before I was born. Jack and I had driven across the bridge a few months ago after I performed an inspection of the Naval Station on Staten Island. Now it's a rusted heap of metal.

In a few minutes we came upon what used to be the Battery, the southernmost tip of Manhattan Island. It looked like the cover of a dystopian novel. The Freedom Tower, the proud replacement for the Twin Towers that fell on 9/11, had been taken low by a nuclear explosion. It once stood at a skyscraping

1,776 feet. Now it couldn't be more than 200 feet high. It was surrounded by small hills of wreckage.

When we looked to port, we could see the tower on which the Statue of Liberty once stood. It was now just a tower, or rather half a tower. Part of it had crumbled to the ground. A huge hill of vegetation covered what was once, presumably, the Statue of Liberty herself. Oh, my God. The most iconic symbol of America is now just a pile of junk.

"Admiral Patterson, this is Commander Philips in Air Ops. Please look at what one of our drones is picking up."

I looked at the video monitor and saw a pack of wolves scampering through the wreckage. Yes, a pack of wolves—in Manhattan.

"I wonder what they eat," Jack said.

"I don't even want to think about that at the moment."

"Admiral, look at the top of the screen at about two o'clock," Phillips said.

A small herd of sheep munched on patches of vegetation. "Looks like the wolves are about to have lunch," said the OOD.

"Thank you, Commander," I said to the air boss. "Let me know if you pick up anything else." No way in hell did I want to see the wolves chowing down on the sheep. We slowly proceeded north up the Hudson. I was surprised by the depth of the water, not as shallow as I'd expected. But I was starting to learn not to expect anything, just observe and record.

Jack and I own (*own or once owned?*) a townhouse in Manhattan, a lovely six-bedroom place on Fifth Avenue with a stunning view of Central Park, bought by Mr. Moneybags Jack before we married. I grew up in the borough of Queens, just over the East River. It was sickening to see what had become (will become?) of the city we loved.

"Commander," I said to the air boss, "increase altitude on the drones so we can get a wider view."

Manhattan was a wasteland, as simple as that. I saw what might have been the Empire State Building at one time but was now just a small mountain of wreckage. Around the midtown area, we could see the outline of a crater, obviously from a bomb that exploded near the ground. The skyscrapers that gave Manhattan its once beautiful vistas were now part of a wolf-infested forest. I wiped some sweat from my forehead. I ordered the drone to fly up the East River.

As we passed what would have been 54th Street, Jack and I looked at each other. Our beautiful brownstone on Fifth Avenue and 54th Street was somewhere out there in the ruins and forest. Not long ago, Jack and I hosted a small cocktail party for my Strike Group captains at our brownstone while the Group was docked in New York. I recalled walking along Fifth Avenue, heading toward our house. That was only a month ago. A month ago? How about 209 years and one month?

We continued north toward the George Washington Bridge. From a distance of two miles, we could see that the roadway had collapsed. Both towers were still erect, along with the graceful suspension cables. Apparently, the open structure of the towers' frames enabled them to withstand the shockwaves of the bomb blasts. The vertical cables that once held the roadway were now rusted tendrils and swayed gently in the light wind.

I ordered the drone to fly across Manhattan to Queens. I wanted to see the Bronx-Whitestone Bridge. There it was, both towers still standing, along with both suspension cables. The roadway had collapsed, and the cables hung free, just like the

George Washington Bridge. I turned toward Jack.

"I grew up a half mile from that bridge in Whitestone," I said softly, tears streaming down my face. Not very command-like. Fuck it. This was my home, the place where I grew up. Now it's in ruins.

In my position, it's important to keep up appearances, a display of military leadership. When you're in charge, it's important to show the troops that you have the situation in hand, to put on a poker face that says, "I have this under control." And now I have a whole strike group counting on me. I felt like crying, but I held it in to keep up a semblance of command appearance. To see the city where you grew up turned into a forest inhabited by wolves is not a pleasant way to spend your morning.

Jack looked at me, reached out, and held my hand. I guessed it was obvious that I was an emotional wreck. Jack knows instinctively when I need to feel his touch.

"Jack, honey, we've got to put an end to this shit. The mission of CSG 3400 has suddenly changed. We've got to get back to 2021 and sound the alarm, along with all the other captains in the group. Hopefully, people will listen to us, unlike the assholes at Pearl Harbor and Midway. Let's head back to Long Island, or *The Island* as it's now called. We need to pick the fertile brain of Bill Wellfleet, our *Keepers of Time* friend, and then weigh anchor for 2021. Please sound the order, baby."

Chapter 17

When we arrived at the spot off *The Island*, I ordered all the ships of CSG 3400 to drop anchor near the compound of Bill Wellfleet and his *Keepers of Time* people. We all headed to shore in our launches. My launch had the charming name, the "Admiral's Barge." The Navy is better at winning wars than it is at giving things appropriate names. Take it from me, a woman who lives in a part of the ship called "Admiral's Country." Go figure. Before we headed for the wormhole to 2021, I realized that Bill Wellfleet had a lot more to tell us. Bill led us to one of the larger buildings in the complex. Although it and the other buildings were totally modern, they had a quaint beauty, as if from the 19th Century. These *Keepers* people are a classy group, and we're about to find out who they are and why they carry the strange name, *The Keepers of Time.*

We were all led into a large conference room. As it was getting close to supper time, we figured it would be a meal meeting. Jenny, typically, offered her assistance to the *Keepers* people in serving the food. Jenny has, in equal measure, brains and kindness.

Bill Wellfleet, looking his Brooks Brothers best, stood at the front of the room next to a viewing screen to show some video clips and still photos.

"I'm about to tell you about *The Keepers of Time*. You can also read about in a book I wrote, titled, of course, *The Keepers of Time*. You can buy it from Amazon and download it to your Kindle. Yes, Amazon and the Kindle still exist in the year 2230.

"Before I tell you about *The Keepers of Time* let me first summarize for you what your eyes have just seen, the results of *The Great War Crisis*. I'm about to discuss the single most important event of the past 209 years. We've given you pieces of information, and a lot of it you already know from the cruise we just took to New York City. Now I'm going to concentrate on the run-up to the war, and the first few years after it. The most important two words that I can think of, and I've written a book on the subject, is 'underestimate,' as in 'never underestimate the intentions of your enemy.' The second word is 'intelligence.' When you have active intelligence, don't ignore it."

Intelligence—what a concept! I wished Bill Wellfleet could have spoken to the shitheads in command at Pearl Harbor and Midway. They could have had *a meeting*.

Bill removed his jacket and stood before the group.

"In the latter days of *PWT* or Pre-War Time, the United States was busy gathering intelligence on the Islamic Republic of Iran. The two nations, and you know this part, had signed a Nuclear Arms Accord in 2015, along with six other countries led by the United States. The deal limited Iran's ability to enrich uranium to bomb grade in exchange for a gradual easing of sanctions by the United States and its allies. Uranium that is mined from the earth is less than 1 percent U-235, the isotope used to fuel reactors and make bombs. Centrifuges are needed to separate the U-235 from the other part of the uranium, in a process called enrichment.

The other fuel that can be used to make a bomb, plutonium, is made by irradiating uranium in a nuclear reactor. The process transforms some of the uranium into plutonium. During enrichment, centrifuges were used to raise concentrations of U-235. For most power reactors, such as the one that drives your ship, the *Ford*, uranium is enriched up to 5 percent. Bomb grade is above 90 percent and Iran had been processing uranium ore to a 20 percent enrichment level, or so the American government thought. You Americans believed you had your shit together, but obviously you didn't. The whole objective, from the West's point of view, was to limit Iran's ability to make bombs. The way to achieve that objective, the United States leadership believed, was careful inspections and monitoring, emphasis on the word careful. As I'm about to discuss, the United States wasn't careful enough."

"The agreement called for some pretty strict limits on centrifuges, if I recall," Jack said. "From what you're saying, Iran simply ignored the limits?"

"Yes, the huge uranium plant at Natanz was limited to five thousand centrifuges, about half of its pre-agreement level. In the year after the accord, the United States complained of numerous violations of the agreement by Iran. An Iranian scientist who survived the war confirmed that Iran used its plant at Natanz as a waving flag. The thinking of the Mullahs was that if you keep the Americans busy with numerous. small violations, it would free Iran for bigger projects, and that's exactly what happened. It had been in planning two years prior to the signing of the deal. The Iranians had a well-known reputation in the West for duplicity, for out-and-out lying. Israeli Prime Minister, Benjamin Netanyahu, called the agreement a 'historic mistake,' one that would create a 'terrorist nuclear superpower.' Netanyahu proved to be prophetic. What Iran managed to pull off was the most amazing ruse in the history of man.

While the United States and its allies busied themselves with inspections at Natanz, Iran was creating an even bigger facility right nearby, about twice the size of Natanz. The uranium enrichment went on unobstructed. By then, the centrifuges spun at a 90 percent uranium enrichment point—the bomb making level. Unknown to American intelligence, Iran and North Korea had begun a process of cooperation that would bring the world as it then existed to an end. North Korea, while millions of its citizens suffered from malnutrition, managed to buy 50 nuclear weapons on the black market that resulted after the fall of the Soviet Union, and then obtained another 85 nukes from Iran."

"Can you tell us anything about the delivery of the bombs?" I said.

"Yes, Admiral," Bill continued. "The West assumed that without inter-continental ballistic missiles, ICBMs, a hostile power would be limited to suitcase nuclear bombs. Both Iran and North Korea realized that there was a much easier way to deliver a large number of nuclear weapons. The answer was nuclear bombs delivered by truck. The weapons were detonated by a signal from space, from the same satellites used to create wormholes."

"So, what you're saying, Bill, is that the *Wormhole Crisis* is a part of what will become the *Great War Crisis*."

"That's correct, Admiral. The *Wormhole Crisis* and the *Great War Crisis* are one and the same. North Korea did not have satellites, so they sent the coordinates of the truck locations to Iran. North Korea also delivered bombs by short-range missiles launched from freighters. North Korea was completely destroyed in the exchange that followed, after it was attacked by the United States, with an assist from South Korea. China decided to look the other way. China was not fond of its unstable 'ally,' North Korea."

"Bill, God knows we just saw what happened to New York," I said. "Can you summarize what happened to the rest of the world?" The captains of CSG 3400 sat there, mesmerized by the horror that Bill Wellfleet described. I looked across the room at the bathroom door, calculating how long it would take me to get there and throw up.

"It was definitely a World War, Admiral. London was totally devastated, as well as Paris, Rome, Madrid, Berlin, Washington, and, as you just saw, New York. Except for the few bombs delivered by North Korea on small ships, all the bombs were delivered by truck and detonated by the wormhole-creating satellites. The United States ceased to exist.

"Although once protected by its vast spaces, Russia lost its central government and returned to a pre-Czarist state. It's now controlled by small units, similar to *the towns* in what used to be America. The United States retaliated against Middle Eastern countries, ironically helped by Russia to the extent of its ability. The Iranians achieved the 'end of days' conflagration they were looking for. The capital city, Tehran, was destroyed, as well as the Holy City of Qum, and Kharg Island. The country is no longer a state but a lawless region similar to the tribal rule areas of the Dark Ages. They use the ancient name to refer to what's left—Persia. Before the breakdown in the compliance talks, American intelligence had also focused on Syria, of course, and then on Libya, both strongholds of that barbaric group called the Islamic State or ISIS. The retaliation against those countries was also massive. One could argue that Israel got lucky. Only one bomb was detonated in the country in a relatively unpopulated area. Historians have identified navigational errors as the reason that Israel was spared. But Israel was by then a sole outpost of civilization in a lawless region, an outpost without the friendship of its now powerless protector, the United States. During and after the war, Israel was attacked repeatedly by conventional weapons."

"So was any country or countries left standing?" Jack asked.

"Yes, Jack," said Wellfleet, "China, Japan, and South Korea, now simply known as Korea, survived and prospered—well, prosper is a relative term—to this day. If there's any such thing as a superpower, it's definitely China. Within 10 years after the war, China abandoned communism entirely, and is an active trading partner of all of the countries of Asia. Oh yes, I should add, Taiwan is now part of China. They reunited after Taiwan realized that the old animosities caused by communism no longer existed."

"Are any of these countries active in what used to be America?" Jenny said.

"It depends on what you call *active*," said Wellfleet. "For the first 10 years after the war, they apparently ignored the West. The ruling policy over 200 years appears to be that the West and the Middle East created the problem that led to the war, so now they must live with it. But *The Keepers of Time* has a very good relationship with China and the other countries of Asia. I will never forget the day, 15 years ago, when a gentleman named Mi-Ki Chung appeared on the doorstep of the Greenbrier, our main headquarters. I'll tell you more about Greenbrier shortly. We call him 'Mickey,' and communicate with him regularly. The purpose of his visit, on behalf of the government of China, was to inquire if they might have access to some of our vast database of knowledge.

I'll never forget his reaction when I said 'Sure, what would you be willing to pay for our services?' Without batting an eye, Mickey said $10 million, in the equivalent of the old American dollar. Inflation has hardly existed since the *Great War Crisis*, so $10 million was a wonderful sum. Mickey couldn't believe that we were willing to share our database. I didn't want him to renege on his offer, so I didn't explain to him that our mission is to disseminate the records of history—without charge, not to keep it hidden. So, his offer couldn't be described as a payment, more like a gift. We're hooked up via an old cross-Pacific fiber optic cable connected to land lines that still exist. It did require some trenching on land, but China was happy to foot the cost. I know you will want to ask this question, whether China has launched any satellites. The answer is yes, they have about 100 satellites in space. China is the only country with rocket technology to enable a space launch. I think that soon they'll see no risk in opening satellite access to the world. In the near future the old Internet will be resurrected, and worldwide communications will be back to where it was—209 years ago. So, China is still very much a superpower, but a peaceful and responsible one with a growing democracy."

"Whatever became of radical Islam? Does it still exist?" Commander Betty asked.

"The religion of Islam still exists," Wellfleet said, "but what was known as radical Islam died on the vine after the war, or rather it was killed. In the lawlessness that existed in the few years postwar, worldwide rage centered on radical Islam. Muslims, even quiet, peaceful Muslims, were hunted down and killed. Mosques were destroyed, and virtually any vestige of the radical elements were dead. But the horrors of the radical fringes of Islam lived on, although in a purely secular way. The barbarians who created the towns adopted the worst parts of the once-hated Islamist fringe.

At this point I should discuss the gladiatorial stadiums

that exist in each of the barbaric towns. Yes, you heard me, *gladiatorial*. The leadership of the brutal towns realized that they needed to keep their citizens distracted and entertained, lest they become restless. So, they built the stadiums, which became savage killing grounds, with young people battling to death before throngs of bloodthirsty spectators. We have a video, taken recently, of two pretty young women squaring off at each other with swords. The taller of the two swung her sword, decapitating the other woman. The crowd screamed in delight. The towns encourage the gladiators and gladiatrixes to fight by kidnapping their loved ones. It's a question of fight in the arena or see your loved ones die. Make no doubt about it folks, outside the areas controlled by the *Keepers* there is nothing but primitive savagery.

The gladiatorial stadiums, when not in use for combat entertainment, are used for spectacles of death by stoning. Yes, believe it or not, stoning to death still exists. We have a video taken recently at the Eastern Empire stadium. It showed a young woman, buried in sand up to her shoulders, being stoned to death by an enthusiastic gang of 12 men, as the crowd in the stadium cheered them on. It took her 15 minutes before she stopped moving. Then one of the men walked up to the pit and hurled a large rock at her head, finishing her off. The offense for which she was killed? Adultery. Her 78-year-old *assigned* husband accused her of having an affair with a young man, although he presented no evidence other than his words. The accused young man was stoned to death the following morning.

Gladiatorial fights are scheduled for afternoons, and mornings are allocated for stoning. Besides death by stoning, the town barbarians have also adopted the old radical Islamist punishments of cutting off the limb of a person accused of stealing. So yes, radical Islam is dead, but the reason people hated and feared it lives on. My heart goes out to the peaceful Muslims who want nothing more than to worship in peace."

"What is the current population of the world, if you have any idea, Bill?" I asked.

"Admiral, prepare to be shocked," said Bill. "In the year you came from, the world population was estimated to be 7.3 billion people, with 330 million in the United States. Now, and of course the figures are far from exact, we estimate the population of the world to be 900 million, with the former United States having been depleted from 330 million to 25 million. The world has shrunk substantially in the past 209 years."

"My God," I said, "is that because of the *Great War?*"

"Yes," said Wellfleet, "either directly or from its consequences over the past two centuries. The mass devastation of the bombings caused millions of deaths. Over the next five years many millions succumbed to radiation poisoning, and cancer deaths from radioactivity continued for decades. But there was, and *is*, an even bigger problem: fertility. Genetic mutations resulting from the worldwide fallout over the years caused changes in the ability of most women to reproduce. It began in the years after the war and has accelerated every year.

"Just this morning I was with a group of people as a young pregnant woman walked down the path. We all applauded because it's a wonderful sight, and a rare one—a woman expecting a child. The fertility rate worldwide simply isn't anywhere near the replacement level. That fact only adds to the insanity of the towns' sacrificing the lives of young people of child-rearing age in the gladiatorial arenas, people who just may be fertile. I hope I'm not being overdramatic when I say that the human race could be facing extinction."

I decided to call a well-needed break. After seeing the devastation of New York City, followed by Bill Wellfleet's description of the *Great War* and its horrible aftermath, we all needed to chill, if only for a short time. Jack and I found an alcove that was empty of people. We hugged. Sometimes words aren't needed, and a hug from Jack always fills the bill. Whatever shit life throws my way, at least I have my Jack to steady me. He kissed me on the lips as he gently stroked my ass. I didn't want to let him go, but it was time for the meeting to resume.

After the break, I stood at the front of the room.

"So, we've just learned that the *Wormhole Crisis* is much more than a crisis involving wormholes, but of satellites that can detonate nuclear weapons from space. That led to the *Great War*, and the end of the world as we knew it."

The mood in the room could best be described as glum. Jenny raised her hand, a broad smile on her face. I could tell that she had a mood-changing icebreaker up her sleeve, as only Jenny can deliver.

"Why are elephants so wrinkled, Admiral?" Jenny said.

"I give up. Why?" This should be good.

"Because they don't fit on an ironing board."

The room broke out in hysterical laughter. God bless Jenny. She knows just how to lighten the mood with her humor.

After the laughing stopped, I asked Bill Wellfleet to come to the front of the room.

"Folks, our friend Bill Wellfleet will now tell US all about *The Keepers of Time*, who they are and what is their mission. "

Chapter 18

So now I'll tell you folks about *The Keepers of Time*," Bill said, "who we are and what's our purpose. I've already mentioned Grandpa Zeke, my four-times great grandfather and the founder of *The Keepers of Time*. Grandpa Zeke, a man from your era of time, is best described as a prepper or survivalist, one who constantly prepares for an unknown future. You folks would have thought of him as an eccentric, a loony nut job. Well, he may have been somewhat crazy, but thanks to him we still have a vestige of civilization—the areas controlled by the *Keepers*.

After the *Great War*, Grandpa Zeke saw what was happening to civilized society. The barbarians who ran the towns couldn't have cared less for what society had become. Literacy was only a sometimes thing, and the idea of studying history was an anathema to those savages, who would rather spend their time watching gladiatorial combat than reading history. Grandpa Zeke realized that something needed to be done about the rapidly disappearing society. Some things needed to be kept alive, the rudiments of what was once a thriving civilization. Time itself, Grandpa Zeke realized, needed to be preserved, to be kept. Hence, he came up with *The Keepers of Time,* an organization pledged to preserving what should be preserved. It wasn't just a matter of preserving the past, but of keeping its most essential remnants. Thanks to Grandpa Zeke, we have an antidote to the primitive savagery of the barbaric towns. How can civilization be preserved is the question. *The Keepers of Time* is the answer."

"Bill, you mentioned earlier that your main location is the Greenbrier," Captain Fletcher of the *USS Knox* said. "Could you explain that please?"

"The Greenbrier is the beautiful resort, founded in 1778 in White Sulphur Springs, in the Allegheny Mountains of West Virginia. In the time you come from it was thriving, and it still thrives to this day. Thank God it was spared in the *Great War,* probably because nobody thought that bombing a resort was important. The expanded site is huge, thanks to the *Keepers of Time,* and the current version covers 34 square miles, about the size of Manhattan.

The main building of the Greenbrier can only be described as beautiful. It's a sprawling, gracious southern mansion. We have other outposts of the *Keepers* scattered around the world, but the Greenbrier in West Virginia is definitely the center of things and is the command post. The Greenbrier was once reserved as an emergency relocation seat of the American government in case the leadership was required to vacate for some reason, such as a nuclear attack. The operation was known by its code name, Project Greek Island. That function was ended in 1992 after it became public in a newspaper story. No sense trying to keep secret what's no longer a secret. Fortunately, the bombs of the *Great War* didn't target the Greenbrier, and it was spared. I would love the opportunity to have you folks as guests at the Greenbrier. The food is wonderful, the accommodations luxurious, and it also has a few excellent golf courses."

Bill Wellfleet's stories were fascinating, and I could listen to him forever, but my mind kept wandering to a different time and place. According to Bill, the *Great War,* the great *nuclear* war, will begin on April 13, 2022. Today is May 15, 2021, which means the world will end less than a year from now. Time to stop listening and to do something. Without exaggeration, our mission now is to save humanity. How's that for a duty assignment?

"How do you protect yourselves from those terrible towns?" Betty Parker asked.

"Let me put it this way." Bill said. "If you want to commit suicide, pick a fight with the *Keepers*. We maintain a sophisticated and powerful military, patterned on the original United States Marine Corps. No primitive towns are a match for our military power."

"Bill, I know that I speak for everyone here when I thank you for letting us know what we're going to be confronted with." I said. "My job, *our* job, is to convince President Blake that we need to take action—*NOW*. I do hope that Jack and I can take you up on your offer to visit the Greenbrier someday, but now I need to address the fact that a nuclear war looms in front of us—the expanded *Wormhole Crisis*. Folks, I'm about to give the most important order of my life, and I don't think any of you will disagree. It's time to weigh anchors, cross the wormhole, go to Washington, and raise hell. I say raise hell because that's what we're faced with. Please return to your ships and prepare to get underway. Carrier Strike Group 3400 has a critical mission to perform—to prevent the end of the world."

Chapter 19

The ships of Carrier Strike Group 3400 weighed anchor this morning at 0800. We bade farewell to our dear friends from the 19th Century, Captain Nigel Kingsmith and First Lieutenant Jeremy Campbell. Our new wormhole detection devices, our *Wormies,* gave me hope that we may see them again.

At 0913, the *Ford* passed through the wormhole off *The Island,* followed by the *Garcia,* the *Knox,* the *Bronstein,* and the *Oliver Hazard Perry.* Our *Wormies,* coupled with our skilled helmsmen, made the task easy. We planned to anchor in the Potomac near Washington, D.C.

Jack, as always, had secured us clearance to drop our anchors. He also arranged for all of us to meet with President Blake at the White House. With Jack, things don't just happen, he makes them happen. How can I accomplish anything without my Jack?

At 0845 we were escorted into the conference room next to the Oval Office. All five captains of CSG 3400 were there along with, of course, the original *Wormhole Gang,* Jack, Jenny, Mike, and me. My heart occupied its usual place in my body—my stomach. With everyone's agreement, I told the President our story. At my request, Jenny had prepared a four-by-four-foot poster on a stand to serve as a backdrop for my talk. The poster simply read, "April 13, 2022. *The Day the World Will End.*"

I told *THE STORY*, emphasizing that the *Wormhole Crisis* involves a lot more than wormholes. I began with our time trip 209 years into the future. I didn't need to explain time travel to President Blake. After constant interactions with Jack and me, he gets what time travel is, as well as any of us gets it. I told him of our sickening trip to New York City, and spent a lot of time talking about *The Great War Crisis,* a nuclear conflict that will happen in less than a year, a war that will bring the world as we know it to an end. I discussed in detail how Iran violated its agreement, expanded the deadliness of the wormhole satellites, and actually started the war. I also spoke about the barbarity that became of the world after the war, including the gladiatorial stadiums, where innocent young people sacrificed their lives. The President looked like he was about to throw up. I also explained, on a more pleasant note, *The Keepers of Time,* an organization that had become the only remaining vestige of civilization. Throughout my talk, many of my expanded *Wormhole Gang* weighed in with their comments.

Jenny raised her hand and I called on her.

"Admiral Ashley, why don't we make the President's job easier and tell him exactly what we want to achieve here today?"

As usual, Jenny focused on the most critical issue.

"Mr. President," I said, "it's no surprise that your cousin zeroed in on the most important issue. So here is our objective, sweet and simple. We've got to stop the war before it starts, which is less than a year from now. Just how to achieve that we leave to your brilliant skills of diplomacy."

The President stood and walked to the large window which overlooked a garden. He is well known for his habit of pacing his office when he has a decision to make. First Lady Dee remained seated. She knows instinctively when her husband needs to climb inside his brain.

He walked back to the front of the room, his hands in his pockets. I've known him long enough to recall that having his hands in his pockets means he's nervous.

"Ashley, I've known you and Jack for a long time and if there is one thing I can say about the both of you is that I believe every word out of your mouths. You two are a couple of the finest Americans there are. And, as my brilliant cousin pointed out, this meeting has one purpose—to prevent the coming war. Yes, I fully believe what you've said about the war, and, needless to say, it's horrifying.

"But we have a problem, a big one. I'm sure it comes as no surprise to you as military leaders, but this is not something the United States can take on by itself. I need to round up all of our allies, some of whom are only *possible* allies. You don't need to be a lawyer to understand the concept of hearsay evidence. Basically, hearsay evidence is presented by a witness who heard the evidence from *someone else*. The problem is that you can't cross-examine someone who picked up knowledge second-hand, which is why a judge will never allow hearsay evidence to be presented in a courtroom.

"And the same idea holds true in the arena of diplomacy, maybe even more so than the law. Not trusting the other guy is a basic tenet of international negotiations. Sure, you hope that negotiations will be conducted with good will, but good will takes a second seat to trust, or the lack of it. So, what you folks have said today is believable, at least to me, and is shocking as hell. But I can't go to other governments and ask them to believe second-hand evidence. They will want to hear from the source of the information, not from hearsay. Which brings me to this fellow you discussed, Bill Wellfleet. Ashley, what are your chances of bringing him here to his past?"

"Mr. President, Wellfleet is a serious, thoughtful man, totally dedicated not only to peace but to preserving civilization. Bill's four-times great grandfather, Ezekiel Wellfleet, lives at the Greenbrier Resort in West Virginia. Not only is he the man who saw it happen, he's the one who started *The Keepers of Time.* I'm sure that I can convince Bill Wellfleet to visit us in 2021. I don't doubt that he will ask Grandpa Ezekiel Wellfleet to be here as well."

"Ashley, go for it," the President said. "We have a war to stop."

Chapter 20

It made no sense to take the entire Strike Group on our next trip through time, so I decided we'd take the *Ford* alone. I could have chosen one of the smaller ships from CSG 3400, but I realized that we may need aircraft. I called my old friend, Betty Parker, CO of the *USS Oliver Hazard Perry*. I asked her to accept the role of Assistant Executive Officer of CSG 3400, and I wanted her to be part of our trip. She will serve right behind Jack. I could have simply given Betty an order, but she's an old friend so a request seemed more appropriate. I never let friendship stand in the way of duty, and conversely, I'm cautious not to let duty automatically conflict with friendship. She readily agreed and turned over command of the *Perry* to her executive officer. Betty was invested in stopping this crisis as much as I was. She recommended that we invite the other captains of CSG to join us on the *Ford* for our trip to Washington, and I agreed.

Captain Luke Barrett, Commanding Officer of the *Ford*, had come down with a wicked case of pneumonia and was in no shape to travel, through time or otherwise, so I took command of the *Ford*.

We steamed to Eastern Long Island and the wormhole to the year 2230. Jack stood next to me on the bridge, holding the wormhole detection device, the *Wormy*, as we approached the target. I glanced at the beeping *Wormy* and there it was, the coordinates of the wormhole dead ahead. We felt the familiar rumbling and the daylight turned dark. My God, the *Wormy* makes crossing a wormhole as easy as walking through a door.

When we emerged on the other side, there was Long Island, or *The Island* as it's known over 200 years into the future. So, *The Gang* boarded the launch and headed for shore. Betty Parker took command of the *Ford* in my absence. The person at the welcome desk told us that Bill Wellfleet had returned to *Keepers* headquarters at the Greenbrier in West Virginia. I called ahead to let Bill know we were coming. He sounded happy as a pig in shit. He had become fond of us, and during our time together and we liked him as well. I didn't tell him the purpose of our trip—to bring him back in time to meet President Blake. I figured that an in-person request was called for. From what President Blake said, it's absolutely essential that Bill Wellfleet join us in Washington to help the President round up allies. I also wanted to check out the Greenbrier, the outpost of civilization.

We steamed for the Delmarva Peninsula where we'd drop anchor in Delaware Bay and fly to the Greenbrier in West Virginia. We used the COD (Carrier Onboard Delivery plane) for the 275-mile flight to White Sulphur Springs. The Greenbrier was a 20-minute car ride from the Greenbrier Valley Airport. Bill said he would meet us at the airport.

Wellfleet picked us up in a beautiful Rolls Royce limo. The car was a 2018 model, making it over 200 years old, even though it looked brand new. I experienced one of my time travel moments. My God, these *Keepers* people are talented at preserving things. He also ordered a huge SUV to accommodate the captains of CSG 3400. Next to the limo was a heavily armed Jeep with an

M2 Browning, a 50-caliber machine gun, mounted on the roof. I asked Bill what the firepower was all about, and he reminded me about what he'd told us before, that the primitives in the year 2230 are not friendly, to say the least. When not sacrificing young people in the gladiatorial stadiums, they happily raid travelers on the roads, murdering and pillaging. But they have learned, the hard way, not to pick a fight with the *Keepers*. If you do that, you've committed suicide.

In 20 minutes, we pulled up to the main building of the Greenbrier. Jack and I were shocked, more like stunned. We had been to the Greenbrier a few years ago for a conference. It was amazing that nothing had changed, *in over 200 years*. The building looked exactly as we had seen it before. Even the landscaping looked the same. The land area was much bigger, but that seemed to be the only difference. *The Keepers of Time* definitely earn their title.

Bill took all of us, the original *Wormhole Gang* along with the captains of CSG 3400, on a fascinating tour of the Greenbrier. He showed us the famous Bunker, which was once the alternate seat of government in case of a national disaster.

"This looks like the floor of Congress," Jack said.

Like the rest of the world, everyone at the Greenbrier wore their COVID-19 face masks and kept a social distance of six feet from other people. We insisted on this precaution and the Greenbrier folks readily agreed. I hated the idea that we might inadvertently bring the virus to the 23rd Century.

He then took us on a tour of the meeting rooms which were almost countless. This place is designed for getting things done, and it's clear that these *Keepers* like to get things done.

Then he took us to his office where he introduced us to his wife, Magda, a lovely woman about my age I figured, after making an adjustment of 200 years. Magda had a background in the theater and couldn't seem to let go of her stage personality. She swept into the room, referring to us all as "Dahlings." Magda was the director of the *Keepers of Time* theater company, yet another vestige of civilization the *Keepers* keep alive.

Although I was antsy to get back to Washington, Bill convinced us to stay that night for a performance of *The Sound of Music*, put on by the theater company. Magda played the part of Maria von Trapp, the heroine, once memorably performed by Julie Andrews. I've always been a fan of beautiful singing, but I was mesmerized, as were all of us, by Magda's amazing voice. In my head I can still hear her singing, "*The hills are alive with the sound of music....*" There are worse things in life than hanging around with *The Keepers of Time*. Magda begged me to take her with us on our return trip through time, and no way could I refuse. Both Magda and Bill wanted to visit Bill's four-times great grandfather, Ezekiel Wellfleet. So, it took me very little persuading to convince Bill to come to Washington. If we were in the same period of time, I could have simply made a phone call. He was that anxious to join us.

As we boarded the *Ford*, the officer of the deck announced, "Carrier Strike Group 3400, arriving." Bill looked at me and said, "Wow, you really are the boss, aren't you?"

Jack and I took the Wellfleets on a tour of the *Ford*. We were amazed that they already knew almost everything about the ship. There is very little that the *Keepers* don't study.

As we crossed the wormhole, Bill and Magda seemed perfectly comfortable traveling 200 years to the past. They got a big kick out of our *Wormy*, the wormhole detecting device. I promised that I will get them a few *Wormies* from the Department of Defense. It was starting to become obvious that the *Keepers* are our allies, our close allies, not to mention just plain good friends.

Chapter 21

Jack arranged for Bill and Magda to stay at Blair House, the White House guest residence. President Blake was in Berlin for a NATO conference, and he wasn't due to return to Washington for four more days.

"Since we have some time on our hands," Bill said, "how about we go to the Greenbrier and visit Grandpa Zeke. He'll freak out to see me and Magda. I hope you and Jack can come with us, Ashley."

I loved that Bill used the phrase from our time, "freak out."

"I think your Grandpa Zeke is a key to this operation," I said. "Let's head there now. I'll invite the CSG 3400 captains to join us."

Jack called the Navy motor vehicle office and arranged two large SUVs for us. Jenny and Mike, of course, were part of our entourage. I never want to be without my *Wormhole Gang*. The Greenbrier is our next logical destination, and I was on edge. But I was also excited as hell to see the place where *The Keepers of Time* originated, and I looked forward to meeting the eccentric Ezekiel Wellfleet. Jenny, thoughtful as always, baked a batch of her delicious chocolate chip and raisin cookies as a gift for Grandpa Zeke.

After a four-hour drive, we arrived at the Greenbrier at 1300. The place was as beautiful as I remembered, both from our conference there a few years ago, as well as from our recent visit to the 209-year-old-version.

Grandpa Zeke met us in the lobby, along with his wife, Bobbie, a strikingly beautiful blond. When I looked at Zeke, I couldn't believe my eyes. None of us could. He and his four-times great grandson Bill looked almost like twins, even though Zeke was over 200 years older. I called Zeke *Grandpa*, but he doesn't look much older than me. Have I mentioned that time travel is weird? Bill had told us that Zeke and Bobbie met when she interviewed him as a reporter with *The New York Times,* and Bobbie filled in the details. She was writing a feature article about *The Keepers of Time,* a group she found fascinating. She said she also found Zeke fascinating, and to listen to her tell it, *cute as a puppy.* So, they had a journalistic love affair and soon got married. I love romantic stories, and the word romantic definitely applies to these two.

"I should advise you folks that I have a black belt in karate," Bobbie said, "so make sure not to call me Grandma." We all cracked up. She has a charming sense of humor as well as beauty.

Zeke and Bobbie took us on a tour of the Greenbrier. It looked the same as it did 209 years into the future. These guys know how to preserve things.

"So, you folks are here to prevent The *Great War,*" Zeke said. I love it when people get right to the point, and that was the point of the meeting, precisely.

"That pretty much summarizes our mission, Zeke," I said. "During our 209-year trip to the future, Bill told us all about the *Great War,* which he predicts will happen less than a year from now. We also visited the future New York City, a post-nuclear wasteland. Besides preventing the war, we are also tasked with putting an end to man-made time travel, which President Blake calls *The Wormhole Crisis.* When we met with Bill, we discovered that the *Wormhole Crisis* is more than just wormholes. The terrorists have figured out a way to direct rays from a satellite and detonate a nuclear bomb on earth. We have our work cut out for us, Zeke."

"I know that Bill has told you all about *The Keepers of Time,*" Zeke said. "From everything I've heard about you folks, Admiral Ashley, it seems that we're on the same team."

"Zeke, honey, why don't we deputize these folks as members of *The Keepers of Time,*" Bobbie said.

"Perfect idea," Jenny said as she clapped her hands. "And we should enroll these guys as members of *The Wormhole Gang.*"

Yes, these *Keepers* people are most definitely our friends and allies.

This meeting was off to a great start. We all agreed that Zeke and Bobbie would accompany us to the upcoming meeting at the White House.

On Wednesday evening we returned to Washington and had dinner at the Oval Room, a classy restaurant right near Blair House, where the Wellfleets were staying. Jack had already reserved a room for Bill and Magda and called ahead to reserve rooms for Zeke and Bobbie. Jack, as always, gets things done. Having dinner with the Wellfleet guys, who looked like twin brothers even though they were over 200 years apart in age, was amazing to say the least. The huge SUVs that Jack had ordered easily accommodated all of us. The next morning, we are scheduled to meet with President Blake. So, Oval Room tonight, Oval Office tomorrow. Jack and I planned to talk until the wee hours, carefully setting up our meeting with the President.

When we returned to our room, Jack stood behind me and hugged me as I was at the bar pouring us wine. I could feel that he was no longer interested in strategic planning. I felt it strongly.

"Hey, handsome, is that torpedo armed?"

"Armed and ready, Admiral. Let me show you just how ready my torpedo is."

Time to go to bed and, maybe, sleep. Making love with Jack helps put all our worries in perspective, especially when his torpedo is armed and ready.

Tomorrow's meeting with President Blake would prove to be the most important meeting of my life, as well as the lives of everyone else. I mean, holy shit, the end of the world is at stake.

Chapter 22

On Thursday, we pulled up to the West Wing of the White House at 8:45 a.m. It was raining like a bitch as we drove under the porte cochère, which was added in 1969, providing some dry protection from the elements. I guessed that before 1969 you only drove up to the West Wing in fair weather. Mike Prentiss, the President's Chief of Staff, greeted us and escorted us inside. I had been to the White House a number of times and was always blown away by its elegance. I'm not sure if it's the physical appearance of the place, or just the knowledge that you are at the seat of world power. Bill and Magda Wellfleet were speechless. Jenny gave her cousin, President Blake, a big hug. She also hugged First Lady Dee. If you wrote an extensive biography of Jenny Blake, the word shy would not appear.

I was surprised, and happy, to see CIA Director Buster and FBI Director Sarah Watson. They and their organizations will be critical to the mission before us. Because of the large number of people, Mike Prentiss escorted us to the conference room near the Oval Office after first letting the CSG 3400 captains snap photos of themselves in the Oval Office.

We all took our seats. The subject of the meeting—saving humanity—kept us all focused. I think of myself as a combat-ready naval warrior, but I was nervous as hell, make that scared out of my mind. We sat six feet apart and removed our masks because we were seated.

I introduced Bill and Magda Wellfleet and asked Bill to take over, after I cleared it with the President.

Bill Wellfleet has a well-honed talent for clear speaking and for summarizing complex subjects. I guess you pick up some useful talent over 200 years. First, he described just who *The Keepers of Time* are and what's their mission. He spoke slowly and deliberately, pausing often for emphasis. Describing the *Keepers* is a bit more complex than describing a Rotary Club. Zeke chimed in with his input. The President seemed blown away about the *Keepers,* peppering Bill and Zeke with nonstop questions.

Next came the stomach-turning subject of the *Great War* and its aftermath, a nuclear war that will happen in less than a year. The President focused on Iran and its nuclear bomb-making capabilities.

"Honey, I mean Mr. President," First Lady Dee said, "Shouldn't we be discussing the wormhole problem, man-made time travel. From what Bill Wellfleet said, there's a critical link between the nuclear war and the *Wormhole Crisis.* Actually, they're one and the same."

The First Lady doesn't hold an official title, but she's a razor-sharp strategist. She may occasionally embarrass herself by calling the President "honey" in public, but Matt Blake doesn't mind. He knows that Dee is his right hand. They remind me of Jack and me.

"Thanks, baby, I mean Madam First Lady," he said with a wink. "I think it's time we heard from our friends at the CIA and FBI. Buster, any comments?"

99

"Mr. President, I'm happy to say that we have some close inside sources at the highest levels of the Iranian government," Buster said. "I know that I can be a pain in the ass with my insistence on a 'need to know,' but I'm sure you understand that I can't mention their names or titles here, other than to you, of course. It's safe to say that we're no longer in the dark about Iranian intentions. I've heard what Bill Wellfleet had to say about the Iranian activities before the coming *Great War*, and he's right on target. But the great news is that we're inside, way inside."

"Buster, there's a reason why your predecessor referred to you as a *super spook*." The President said. "But I want to make it clear that Admiral Ashley, her husband, Captain Jack, and the two Wellfleet gentlemen, have a 'need to know' about this operation. From what I've been told, the end of the world is less than a year away. You need Ashley and Jack and the *Keepers of Time* folks on your side, your deep inner side. We have no time to waste. Make it happen, Buster."

So, typical of him, President Blake set the scene for action. I wish I felt the same way. Although I've accomplished a lot in life, I'm constantly besieged by doubt that I'm doing the right thing. On my way to the door, I glanced at a mirror. *Who the hell is this woman I'm looking at?* With the things I've done, from graduating from the Naval Academy, to achieving the highest rank in the Navy, I too often allow myself to think I'm hot shit. But in my gut, I'm that frightened little girl who worries that I'm doing it all wrong. Jack means everything to me, and I never stop loving him. But do I really love him or am I just pumping myself up because I'm married to a gorgeous specimen? I think it's time for me to really look myself in the mirror and get my act together. Yes, *act*. It's time for me to stop acting and to give a real shit for the people around me. It's time for Ashley Patterson to get real and stop kissing her own ass. I often, too often, tell people that I know how to get the job done. Why don't I just do it and stop bragging about myself? Not a bad idea. It's time to stop the shit and get real. A lot of people depend on me, and it's time I commit myself to giving them a reason. They depend on me to produce results, and that's what I'm going to give them—results.

Kick Ass Ashley has the con.

Chapter 23

Iranian Foreign Minister Farhad Ahmadi sat in his office in Tehran with his friend and associate, Deputy Foreign Minister Hashem Mohammadi. It was a mild, sunny day at 62 degrees and Ahmadi had opened the window a crack to let in the fresh breeze. The office was large at 30 by 50 feet and was elegantly furnished with an assortment of fine leather furniture. Ahmadi makes no secret of his fondness for material luxuries, and he also adorned the walls with original oil paintings, including a couple from the Hudson River School, his favorite school of art. An aide brought in a tray full of seafood snacks. They sat in two comfortable chairs at a small table near the window, which let in a gentle breeze and had a great view of the gardens below.

Ahmadi had worked for the Iranian government ever since he graduated from New York University. He served for five years in the Iranian Army, mustering out with the rank of major. Mohammadi also attended school in America, graduating from Cornell University with a degree in economics. They were friends ever since their teenage years, and they often get together socially along with their wives. They're both Christians, a fact they keep strictly secret, and always celebrate Christmas and Easter together.

Ahmadi walked over to a cabinet, withdrew a bottle of Cutty Sark Scotch, and poured each of them a healthy glassful. Their only major difference was that Ahmadi likes his straight up while Mohammadi prefers scotch on the rocks.

Besides their fondness for scotch, the two men have a lot in common, including their love of chess and American baseball. They're avid fans of the New York Mets, and even figured a way around Iran's blocking of American TV so they could catch games. They also share a deep, festering hatred of the senior officials of the Iranian government, especially Prime Minister Ahura Ghorbani, "that worthless piece of shit," as Ahmadi often describes him. Although they hate the top leadership of their government, they consider themselves patriotic Iranians.

"Hashem, we've got to stop talking and start acting. God knows we have enough allies on our side in the government. The idiots in charge, specifically Prime Minister Ghorbani, are hell bent on destroying our country and taking the world with it. That fool really believes in the insane idea of 'The End of Days.' I sometimes wonder if he's delusional. Sure, the Americans can be clumsy and overbearing at times, but anybody with a brain in his head should realize that America is best thought of as a friend, not an enemy. President Blake is a thoughtful leader, but when provoked, which is what we are doing, he's not hesitant to come out fighting. That outrageous idea of man-made time travel using satellites to create wormholes is the most provocative act imaginable. The Americans thought they had control when they captured our main satellite, but the operation failed. They even put their senior admiral, Ashley Patterson, on the assignment.

Ghorbani dismisses the brilliant Admiral Patterson as if she were an American Girl Scout. Ghorbani believes that women belong in the laundry room or kitchen, not on the bridge of a warship. But, as skilled a military leader as Admiral Patterson is, Iran still has the power to create man-made time travel, and to use the same technology to detonate nuclear weapons from space. Our esteemed Prime Minister seems to think that the United States will keep looking the other way. Nothing could be further from the truth. President Blake knows when his country is being threatened, and no way will he tolerate the threat. And now we continuously violate our agreement to stop creating weapons grade uranium, somehow imagining that the Americans are unaware of what we're doing, or that they don't care. And our alliance with that mad man, Kim Jong-un of North Korea, only furthers the contempt the United States has for us. And it isn't only the United States that is worried about us, but all the peaceful countries of the world. I'm afraid that we have a brain-scrambled maniac as a leader."

"Yes, Hashem, we do have a maniac as a leader, and he's surrounded by highly paid lackeys who do his bidding."

"Farhad, my friend, as you're aware I am in regular contact with our inside man in the States. I believe that my regular communication with him is the only reason the United States hasn't taken some drastic steps against us. I keep nothing from him, and he keeps nothing from me. My God, Farhad, a nuclear war with the United States will be the end of our country, if not the world."

"Farhad, have you spoken recently to this fellow you refer to as 'our inside man?'"

"Yes, Hashem, as recently as yesterday. Don't worry, my friend. As the Americans would put it, *Buster is on the case.*"

Chapter 24

Jack and I, along with the Wellfleet guys, met with Buster in his office at 26 Federal Plaza. Because of President Blake's "need to know" restrictions, the rest of the *Wormhole Gang*, Jenny and Mike, couldn't be with us, much to my disappointment. But orders are orders, whether I like it or not.

We sat around a conference table. If Jenny were there, she would have acted as hostess and served snacks. Buster, always the gentleman, walked around the table and served us coffee. He wore his face mask, of course. The Wellfleets requested tea.

"I can't say I'm happy with the President's decision to expand the 'need to know' doctrine," Buster said. "Don't get me wrong, there are two people in this world who I trust completely, and that is you two, Ashley and Jack. And the fact that you brought your Wellfleet guys to the table gives me trust in them as well. But the 'need to know' doctrine isn't based on trust but on common sense. The more people who know of a secret raises the risk that they may innocently leak information. But forget about my hang-ups. Like everyone else, I follow orders, especially when those orders come from the President of the United States."

"Buster, I'm familiar with the 'need to know rule,' and it makes a hell of a lot of sense," Bill Wellfleet said. "You have nothing to worry about with the *Keepers*. You have my word that I will *keep* my mouth shut."

"I second what my grandson said," Zeke said. "Secrecy is sacred."

Buster cracked up. "I can't get over that you guys are grandson and grandfather, separated by over 200 years. You look like twin brothers. Bill, whatever you eat, I'd like the recipe."

"And you know Jack and me, Buster," I said. "We fully understand that the 'need to know' doctrine comes with a need to keep your mouth shut. I'm sure you know that you don't have to worry about us. As an Admiral, I know a thing or two about secrecy. So, tell us about your mysterious contacts in Iran."

"My contacts are none other than the Foreign Minister and Deputy Foreign Minister of Iran. When I said my contacts are *high officials*, I wasn't exaggerating. I'm sure you will recognize their names. They're often on TV. They are Farhad Ahmadi, Foreign Minister, and Hashem Mohammadi, the Deputy Foreign Minister. You may be surprised to know that they not only confide in me, but it's accurate to say that they are on our side, *deeply* on our side, as are dozens of other highly placed ministers. Yes, they and a lot of other high-ranking people in Iran don't trust that crazy bastard, Prime Minister Ahura Ghorbani. They fully realize that Ghorbani is putting their country at severe risk with his bullshit antics. Ahmadi himself is the source of my knowledge about the wormhole-creating satellite. And what he told me about Iran's nuclear plans conforms exactly to what Bill Wellfleet said, without details about the coming war, of course. So, the good news is that we're inside, deep inside."

"Do we know the exact location of their secondary uranium enrichment facility?" I asked.

"Yes, Ashley, we know exactly where it is, not far from their original facility in Natanz."

"How far below the surface?"

"Pretty deep, about 200 feet."

"Not deep enough to withstand a couple of bunker-buster bombs," I said. "When do you want me to attack?"

Buster laughed. "As always, Admiral *Kick Ass Ashley* wants to get the job done. But it's premature for a bomb strike. President Blake needs to round up some allies first. Also, we're still faced with the problem with the wormhole-creating satellites. As we discovered when we captured and disabled the main satellite, we found out that the wormholes that had already been created still exist. Also, Foreign Minister Ahmadi told me that their plans to construct another wormhole-maker are well under way. Like you, Ashley, I like to pull the trigger, but it's essential that we proceed with caution. And now we learn from the Wellfleets that Iran plans to use the wormhole-creating satellites to detonate nuclear bombs on trucks. My inside people will let me know when we close in on zero hour. If we're in imminent danger, we'll declare war and attack. President Blake has assured me of that. Keep your powder dry, Admiral."

"What about North Korea, Buster?" Jack said. "Do we have insiders in Pyongyang like we do in Tehran?"

"No, we don't have any high-ranking officials talking to us, but we do have an enthusiastic army of spies, *super spooks* as I like to call them. Like me, they don't take any shit. Hell, I trained them. They have that country covered like a blanket. Also, the

North Korean top dogs aren't as careful as the Iranians when they discuss their plans. When they talk, my super spooks take notice and report to me."

"What can *The Keepers of Time* do to assist you, Buster?" Zeke Wellfleet asked.

"We don't see your organization having an active role like Admiral Ashley and her Carrier Strike Group, but you folks are amazing for your well-honed sense of observation. You give new meaning to the word civilization. So, your job is to keep your eyes and ears open. I've only learned about *The Keepers of Time* recently, and I can't say enough how impressed I am with you people. What your organization is all about is what American democracy is all about—freedom and the free sharing of information. It's an honor to work with you guys. Zeke and Bill, when you return to the Greenbrier, I will assign a CIA plane to take you in order to save time. Since Bill is visiting us from 209 years into the future, I'm sure he appreciates saving time."

"Buster, I don't know if you fully appreciate the amount of information we have stored on the *Keepers* computers," Bill said. "Any time you need any research done, just snap your fingers. You will be amazed at what we can dig up in a short amount of time. In a way I haven't figured out yet, I believe the *Keepers* can be a key to your operation."

"I agree with Bill," I said. "The *Keepers* are a vital key for our mission. Something tells me that the *Keepers*, and especially their command center at the Greenbrier, will be a *big part* of our future. I don't know how, but my gut tells me the *Keepers* may become our most valued ally."

"Okay, folks, our meeting today is about over," Buster said. "We're going to get this job done. I'm not exaggerating when I say that the future of humanity depends on us."

Buster knows how to nail a point, and he's right, the future of humanity is in our hands. Holy shit, the future of humanity—not too much pressure.

Chapter 25

Jack and I felt the need to be alone, well not alone, but with each other. Before we return to our charming attack aircraft carrier, which is docked nearby on the West side of Manhattan, we decided to eat at one of our favorite restaurants, L'Aiglon on East 55th Street, not far from our apartment on 54th Street and Fifth Avenue. All the ships of CGS 3400 were docked in New York City, preparing for training maneuvers in the Atlantic.

My sister Terry and her husband, Phil, were in Manhattan for three months to work on a book project. According to Jack, Phil is an excellent writer and Thurber Publishing Company had already launched a couple of his books. They were working on a historical novel centered in New York City at the turn of the 19th Century. The heroine of the book is a female Navy ship captain. How cool is that? They live in London, and we were only too happy to give them our townhouse while they were in the States—because Jack and I now reside on an aircraft carrier. Phil is British and his somewhat cockney accent always reminds me of Paul McCartney. Too bad he can't sing.

The people at L'Aiglon know Jack and me well and try their best to accommodate us on short notice. We sat at one of our favorite tables at the rear of the restaurant, a place bathed in candlelight. It was nestled away from other tables, enabling us to speak without being overheard. Our lives have been nonstop hectic in the past few months, and we felt the need to relax and just be with each other. Being alone with Jack is one of my favorite things in life. We're together all the time, but usually our time with each other involves barking orders at people, making snap command decisions, and all the other bullshit involved with being front-line military. I reached over and stroked Jack's face, something that he loves me to do. It's also something I love to do. He looked adorable in the flickering candlelight. He grabbed my hand and kissed it, then leaned over and kissed me on the lips. We need to do this more often. Being involved in solving a crisis that could see the end of the world is no way to relax. But, just for tonight, we put the crisis on hold and focused on each other. I'm with my Jack, and to me that's the most important thing in the world. Have I mentioned how much I love him?

I looked up and who did I see approaching our table but Sarah Watson and her husband, Harry. She had mentioned that she would be working for a few days out of her New York office at 26 Federal Plaza. Sarah is one of my favorite people, but the last thing I wanted to talk about was FBI stuff. Hey, Jack and I were there for a romantic dinner. Sweetheart that she is, Sarah patted me on the shoulder and gave Jack a peck on the cheek. "You guys have seen enough of me lately, so I'll let you enjoy your dinner." She and Harry walked toward the front of the restaurant. I'd say that Sarah is a class act, but it's not an act. Pure elegance, that one.

The waiter came to our table with the wine we ordered and read the specials. We both ordered Chilean sea bass, one of L'Aiglon's best dishes. No surprise, Jack and I share the same taste in food, just as we share most things together.

The sea bass was fabulous, one of the best seafood dishes I enjoyed in a long time. People love to tell jokes about Navy food, but it's no joke, and is usually quite good. But it's nothing compared to L'Aiglon. Midway through our meal Jack said, "Hey, let's finish up and get back to the cabin on our cruise ship. I have some ideas about the rest of the evening."

"Cruise ship? Jack, baby, you and I live on a friggin aircraft carrier."

"Nothing wrong with a little fantasy. Hey, we often take her on cruises."

"Wiseass. Let's go. I'm dying to see what you have planned for tonight."

I spend almost all my time with Jack by my side, but I can't get enough of him. Especially when he has *ideas* for the rest of the evening.

Horny Admiral, arriving!

Chapter 26

Iranian Prime Minister Ahura Ghorbani sat in his office with Ahmad Rafshandi, his Deputy Prime Minister. Although he carried the title Deputy Prime Minister, in truth Rafshandi was no more than a mid-level aide to Ghorbani, a lackey in other words.

"Ahmad, tell me about the status of our new wormhole-creating satellite."

"The plans are almost complete, Your Excellency. It should be ready to launch in one month."

"I notice that you said, 'should be ready.' Are you not certain? I am only interested in certainty, not an opinion of something that 'should be.' Do I make myself clear, Ahmad?"

"Yes, sir, quite clear. The satellite will be ready to launch in exactly 30 days."

Rafshandi swallowed hard as he said that. What if the satellite isn't ready to launch? Would his life be in danger? Many subordinates had been killed after lying to the Prime Minister. Like many aides, Rafshandi performed his duties out of fear, not respect. He wondered if the Prime Minister is aware of how many people despise him. Although he forces such thoughts from his mind, Rafshandi carries a deep hatred for his ruler. But he is paid extremely well, and his family is provided for. His brother, Iman, had long ago warned him to just do his job and keep his mouth shut. Iman was murdered last year, and his assailant was never found. Iman was in charge of a project that missed its deadline by a week. Ghorbani is strict about deadlines.

"And now tell me how our uranium enrichment program is performing."

"Our facility near Natanz is performing at maximum capacity, your Excellency. We are enriching vast amounts of uranium at 90 percent, which as you know, sir, is bomb grade." Rafshandi wasn't worried about this report because he knew it was true. Soon, Iran would be making nuclear weapons by the hundreds, a thought that sickened him.

"And are our bomb and missile manufacturing plans moving forward?"

"Yes, sir. Our manufacturing activities are actually ahead of schedule, and we have a secret weapon in our satellites. We can detonate a bomb on the ground with a signal from space. That saves us from the complications of a plane or missile attack. It also provides us with a high level of secrecy."

"Are our North Korean friends behaving as we expect them to?"

"Well, sir, Kim Jong-un, who people refer to as the Supreme Leader of North Korea, is well-known to be unpredictable. I'm not sure if we can trust him."

Ghorbani flung an ashtray across the room, crashing it against a wall, sending his house cat scurrying under a couch. Although Iranians typically avoid keeping house pets, Ghorbani has his own rules for himself. His cat had other ideas.

"Ahmad, now you are telling me that we are *unsure* that we can trust a critical ally. This meeting is over. Report back to me tomorrow about Kim Jong-un. And I don't want to hear what you are unsure about. I only want to know what you're *sure* about. Dismissed!"

Drown in your own vomit, you lowlife piece of shit. I really should stop thinking these thoughts, but it's hard not to. Now, I'm under orders to figure out how we can trust an unpredictable maniac in North Korea. I wish I never gave up my old job as a schoolteacher. Now I'm no more than a lackey to a fucking homicidal maniac.

Chapter 27

Ahmad Rafshandi here

So, I reported today, as ordered, to my esteemed leader, the insane Prime Minister Ahura Ghorbani. He wanted an ironclad opinion of the mental status of Kim Jong-un, the Supreme Leader of North Korea. Without doing any further research I gave him that opinion, that Kim Jong-un is mentally unstable and simply cannot be trusted, not *unlikely* to be trusted, but not at all to be trusted. I didn't worry about giving this report because Supreme Leader Kim is obviously unstable and isn't worthy of a bit of trust. Not difficult to back that opinion up with countless newspaper and magazine articles. Just looking at the man on TV is enough to tell you that he's not in his right mind.

All of us who report to Ghorbani are allocated vacation time and sick leave, although Ghorbani has a reputation for ignoring that regulation and demanding a meeting on a moment's notice. I figured it was worth the risk and advised the personnel office that I would be taking a week off. My wife, Donia, has a sister, Yasamin, who lives in New York. Yasamin has been pestering Donia about visiting her and her husband, Max Hart. I've carefully kept their identity hidden from my esteemed leader because Yasamin's husband, Max, is a highly placed agent with the CIA. If Ghorbani knew that little fact, my life wouldn't be worth one Iranian *rial*, which isn't worth much anyway.

My sister-in-law, Yasamin, is a professor of literature at St. Joseph's College, a small Catholic institution in Patchogue, Long Island. Yasamin and Max are childless and are both age 45. They are a close couple and Yasamin is proud of Max's position as an American intelligence agent, although she keeps that information to herself. Yasamin would be described by most Americans as a patriot who loves her country. But as much as she loves her country, I think Yasamin hates me, an official with the despised regime in Iran, an avowed enemy of the United States. I don't blame her. With what she knows, I'd hate me too.

Besides taking this vacation as much needed R&R, I intend to change Yasamin's opinion of me. My wife, Donia, will be in for a surprise as well, and so will Max. Donia hates Prime Minister Ghorbani—almost as much as I do. When she speaks to me about him, she never mentions his name, opting instead for her favorite nickname for him, "that crazy fuck." Well, that crazy fuck will soon be in for a surprise.

It was a beautiful late spring day, and we visited the Harts at their summer home in Sag Harbor on Eastern Long Island. It's a beautiful place, situated on Noyac Bay. Max had inherited a not-so-small fortune from his late bank president father and knows how to invest money. Donia and I speak perfect English, Donia with an American accent. She was born and raised in Chicago. Our English-speaking is one of the reasons I enjoy visiting Yasamin and Max, even though Yasamin hates me. We arrived in our rental car at 11:45 a.m., just in time for lunch.

For reasons I still can't figure out, I felt an amazing calmness. I don't think of myself as a particularly brave man. Truth is, I think I'm a coward at heart. That may be why I never separated myself from Prime Minister Ghorbani, *that crazy fuck* as my wife calls him. I shouldn't feel calm, because I'm about to make an announcement that will change my life forever, as well as the lives of others, such as Donia, Yasamin, and Max. Not to mention the esteemed Prime Minister Ghorbani.

Max is a high-level spy, or spook as he calls himself. He always tries his best not to divulge his occupation, or specifically what he does for the CIA, but I know from tidbits of prior conversations, that he works closely with CIA Director Charles Atkins, better known to everyone as Buster. From keeping my ears open, I know that Buster values his relationship with Max and receives some of his best secret information from him, especially about Iran.

Donia and her sister set up the table for our lunch. Although they both know how to make Middle Eastern dishes, Yosamin prefers Italian cooking. They prepared hot sausages, spicy meatballs, and three pasta dishes, one of which was a seafood medley. Max handed me a beer and a cigar and invited me down to the dock to see their new boat, a sleek 40-foot Mainship trawler. Painted on the stern was the boat's name—"Spooky."

"So, how is everything at your headquarters in Tehran, Ahmad?" Max can never get the spy out of him, and always asks me about my job as chief aide to the dictator Ghorbani. Whatever I say, I'm sure, will be passed along to CIA Director, Buster, and that's fine with me. It will soon become better than fine.

"Things are quite interesting in Tehran, Max. As you may know, we have been producing uranium at 90 percent at our secret plant. Ninety percent, which, I'm sure you know, is weapons grade. In the past month we have manufactured twenty 25-megaton nuclear bombs, as powerful as a nuke gets.

Ten of the weapons have recently been transferred to North Korea. You can forget about our arms agreement."

Although Max, a master spy, is talented at keeping his emotions hidden, he looked like he was about to fall in the water.

"Ahmad, I can't believe you just told me that. Dear God, you're telling me that Iran has violated our agreement and produced 25 high-powered nukes. And here you are talking about it as if we're colleagues. Have you had a change of heart recently?"

"I had a change of heart a long time ago, Max, but I've recently decided to do something about it. I'm now on your side. Consider me your ally. I love the people of Iran, but I hate the leadership of my country, especially Prime Minister Ghorbani, whom my wife calls 'that crazy fuck.' I should also mention to you that Iran has just completed the manufacture of another wormhole-creating satellite, and it is scheduled to be launched in one month. Ghorbani is intent on seeing the fabled 'End of Days.' I'm not going to let that happen. No way in hell will I let my country destroy itself and the world, which Ghorbani seems bent on doing. As a side benefit, I hope that your wife, my lovely sister-in-law, will no longer hate me."

Max grabbed the edge of the trawler, feeling suddenly dizzy.

"Ahmad, I always thought of you as a nice guy, despite working for that madman who runs your country. After what you just said, I now see you as someone who is about to save the world from a catastrophe. God bless you, Ahmad. My boss, Buster, is working out of his New York office in Manhattan this week and I know that you plan to be in the States for a week. Please join me to see him tomorrow. When I hint to him on the phone what we just talked about, I'm sure he will clear his calendar to see you."

Max called Buster from his cellphone. He told him, in advanced *spook talk*, what I had just said. I could hear Buster scream, "Holy shit! Be here at nine a.m. tomorrow."

Max put his phone into his pocket after he entered a code to prevent anyone but him from accessing the phone.

"Oh, another thing, Ahmad, not a word of this to my wife. 'Top Secret' doesn't begin to describe what you just told me. I will announce to Yasamin, in *very general terms*, that you are now a close advisor. I trust her with all my heart, but the 'need to know' rule means keeping secrets secret."

"You will be announcing it to my wife, Donia, as well. I haven't told her a thing, saving it for today."

Max just shook his head, looking like he just heard something he had a hard time believing. We finished our beers and headed up to the deck for lunch. Suddenly I was ravenously hungry. I think that when you get something off your chest, your stomach is pleased and wants to be rewarded.

"Yasamin, honey, as you know, sometimes I tell you things that are edited for security reasons."

"I know, sweety, and I don't mind at all. I get bored listening to your spook talk. So, what's your big, edited announcement?"

"Yasamin, as an American patriot, you have had some serious misgivings, to put it mildly, about your brother-in-law here. As you've told me often, you hate him. So, here's my announcement, without any specifics. Ahmad is a good man, maybe even a great man, someone who deserves your love and trust, not your hatred. He is now on our side and is one of my closest allies and advisors. I haven't told you much, nor can I, but please don't even repeat to anybody what I just said."

Max and Yasamin are a close couple and believe in each other. They're like Donia and me. After Max made his announcement, Yasamin walked over to me, poured me a beer, leaned over, and kissed me on the cheek. She squeezed my shoulder. "If my Max says you're good, Ahmad, you're good. I officially no longer hate you."

I can't believe that my sister-in-law just kissed me. Obviously, when Max talks, Yasamin listens. I felt great about our new friendship.

I told Donia in detail about my career change. When a couple is as close as us, there's no such thing as a "need to know," although I seldom shared with her my meetings with Ghorbani. But now I need her to know everything about my life. When I told her the details, she hugged me so hard I thought I'd crack a rib. Needless to say, she was delighted by my new relationship with "that crazy fuck."

Chapter 28

I felt great about my decision to change sides. I will no longer be a quiet fucking wimp and let Ghorbani spread his wickedness on my country. For a change I'm going to do what's right. I will no longer be ashamed of my name, Ahmad Rafshandi.

At 9 a.m. the next day, Max and I walked into the Director's office at 26 Federal Plaza.

I had a hard time believing I was in the office of none other than Charles Atkins, aka Buster, the Director of the American Central Intelligence Agency, Ghorbani's sworn enemy. But then Ghorbani collects sworn enemies like trading stamps.

I had heard a lot about Buster, but never had met him in person. I've only seen him on TV, and then only when I was in the States. American broadcasts are strictly forbidden in Ghorbani's Iran. Buster couldn't have been more gentlemanly and gracious. His personality didn't conform to my thinking of a hardnosed spy.

He poured a coffee for me and leaned forward, looking deeply into my eyes.

"Ahmad, from what you and Max just told me, I think our

relationship has seen the dawn of a new day. As you well know, you work for a cruel madman, a guy who is willing to see his country driven into the ground, taking the rest of the world with it. Most of us westerners see 'the End of Days' as a bizarre way of thinking, or of *not thinking*. But for Ghorbani, it's a guiding principle, a weird way of looking at destruction as a positive guide to some sort of insane truth. As CIA Director, I have a plateful of horror in front of me as usual, but Iran's actions with its nuclear program and its wormhole creating satellites are at the top of my agenda. If we can't stop Ghorbani, there will be little else to stop. Ahmad, you have just given us two gigantic pieces of inside information. My God, Iran has ramped up nuclear arms manufacturing in violation of our arms accord. Couple that with its renewed wormhole satellite program and we are looking at the end of the United States, not to mention western civilization. You, Ahmad Rafshandi, just may be the answer to the world's prayers, whether you worship Jesus or Allah. You are a good man, Ahmad, and I can't be happier that you've seen the light."

"Mr. Director…"

"Please call me Buster."

"Buster, I need guidance. In my position I'm familiar with state secrets, but I'm not a spy, and I have no training."

"It's not as complicated as Hollywood movies would have you believe, Ahmad. You will work closely with your brother-in-law, Max. He will give encoded messages to your wife Donia through your sister-in-law, Yasamin. You will respond in code, which we will teach you. Your primary job is to keep your eyes and ears open, which you certainly know how to do. Don't overthink this, my friend. Because of you, God bless you, we can bring an end to the end of the world."

Chapter 29

Jack and I were taking our morning jog and walk on the flight deck of the *Ford*. Whatever happened to romantic settings? I mean, holy shit, a stroll with my honey along the flight deck of a friggin aircraft carrier? It did provide some extra exercise because we needed to sidestep parked F/A-18 Super Hornets. You'll never read something like this in a Harlequin romance novel. Maybe Jack and I should write one of our own.

We were both perspiring like crazy and decided to take a shower—together. Sometimes you need to encourage your mood. It was 0915, a bit early, but the time is always right to make love with Jack. As the water splashed down on us, I bit down on a washcloth to keep my screams of ecstasy from traveling around the ship. Admirals need to be appropriate, even when engaging in wonderful sex. I asked Jack if he thought I was behaving appropriately. He didn't say anything but reached down and gently stroked my love center. I let out a washcloth-tempered scream. I was definitely being appropriate, no?

After we went to bed and made love, we lay there naked, wrapped in each other's arms, trying, if only for a brief time, to forget that our mission is to prevent the end of the world. We reluctantly helped each other get dressed. Time to get back to reality—which sucks at times.

My cellphone rang, reminding me that reality is never far away. I looked at caller ID as Jack adjusted my panties, slowly and tantalizingly.

"Buster, how nice of you to call," I lied. He sounded excited about something and I *tried* to sound excited. If he had called 20 minutes earlier, my excitement would have been apparent.

"Ashley, I need to meet with you and Jack about an important new development. I'm at 26 Federal Plaza today. See you shortly."

Jack and I walked into Buster's office. I felt wonderful, having just enjoyed a morning of wild sex with my honey. A Middle Eastern-looking guy who I didn't recognize was just leaving. We weren't introduced, which I found a bit strange. But then, any time I've ever been in Buster's office, there was always something strange. Spooks are like that. Buster was sitting with Max Hart, one of his top agents, a guy whom I've met a number of times. Max is a nice guy, but typical of a CIA agent, he packs a tight suitcase. Any time I ever talked to him it was always *small talk*. "Max is onto something which has everything to do with our wormhole and nuke mission," Buster said. "I'm not exaggerating when I call this a breakthrough. I don't know if you guys are aware of this, but Max's wife, Yasamin, is the sister of a woman whose husband is the right-hand man to that insane bastard, Iranian Prime Minister, Ahura Ghorbani. The guy's name is Ahmad Rafshandi. You passed him when you came into my office. Someday you will meet him, but now is premature. He carries the title Deputy Prime Minister, but he's really just an aide to Ghorbani, a very close aide, more like a lackey. I've told you about my friendly relationship with Farhad Ahmadi, Foreign Minister of Iran and Hashem Mohammadi, the Deputy Foreign Minister. Well, now we're even deeper inside with our new friend, Ahmad Rafshandi. I mean, holy shit, we're virtually sitting across the desk from our enemy."

———————

I'm an admiral and Jack is a captain, but everybody we talk to lately seems to think we're police detectives. I may as well play along, because Buster won't let up. His announcement about Agent Hart's brother-in-law was interesting as hell I had to admit. So, we have an inside track to the man at the top, the man who's taken it upon himself to wreak terror on the world. Maybe Buster will want me to call in a missile strike on Ghorbani's office. Not a bad idea, but it would be an act of war, and none of us has the power to declare war. Hell, it's a lot easier to lead a Carrier Strike Group through a wormhole than engaging in this spook stuff.

———————

Sometimes Jack and I indulge in a fantasy, usually after making love, about us retiring and buying a little bed-and-breakfast in the boondocks. I can picture every last detail. A two-story six-bedroom place on a lakefront acre of property. A cozy dining room includes a large fireplace, in front of which a Golden Retriever has staked out his spot. On one of the dining room walls is a bucolic Hudson River School painting of a valley with two mountains in the distance. The house has a wraparound porch with old rocking chairs and a beautiful view of the lake. A family of swans had adopted the place, adding to the atmosphere. Not a gun placement or a missile battery in sight. Wouldn't it be nice to serve people and make them happy rather than kill them? That fantasy is buzzing around my head right now. Okay, time to snap out of it. Buster is on a roll.

"Ashley, I want CSG 3400 to steam off the coast of Iran. I've cleared this with the Chief of Naval Operations, Admiral Jake

Wayman."

"Buster, if I steam in the territorial waters of Iran, that could be construed as a provocation and result in the group being attacked. We're talking war, and neither you, I, nor the CNO have the authority to pull that off. Sorry, my friend, I have no problem with engaging in battle, but I insist on orders from the White House to do what you're suggesting."

"Ashley, I've taken the liberty of setting up a meeting for you and Jack at the White House this afternoon. A CIA Gulfstream awaits you at JFK. You will meet with Mike Prentiss, President Blake's Chief of Staff. He's expecting you."

Interesting. We'll meet with Mike Prentiss, not the President. That tells me that some serious shit is afoot. When he steps to the brink of war, the President needs to have that sacred cloak of a thing called *deniability.*

As Jack and I waited for the elevator, I turned to him and grabbed his hand.

"Jack, baby, you often sweetly say that you married well. But I'm afraid that your wife has put you in the crosshairs. You deserve better than me."

"I couldn't possibly deserve better than you, honey. Danger and all, you're my girl. I love you more than you can imagine. How about a kiss." He gently stroked my ass as he said that. Jack can make even an elevator ride romantic. Have I mentioned that he's the man? *My* man.

Chapter 30

At 1545 our Gulfstream landed at Dulles and a staff car took us to the White House. Chief of Staff Mike Prentiss met us at the entrance to the West Wing. He took us to his office, not the Oval Office.

"The President is in California today for a meeting," Mike said.

As I suspected, the purpose of this meeting is intentionally *not* for the President's ears.

"Ashley and Jack, you're about to be given an extremely sensitive assignment for Carrier Strike Group 3400. I know that CIA Director Buster has already briefed you. As you've been told, we have high-ranking officials of the Iranian government on our side. The fact that you've been told that only emphasizes the high regard President Blake has for you. The mission of CSG 3400 is to steam off the shore of Iran, but not to take any provocative actions. However, if any military strike is ordered against you, we will know in advance from our insiders. If that happens, you are authorized to launch a full attack on the Iranian regime by all ships of CSG 3400. That will be preceded by a Declaration of War against Iran, although we don't expect that to happen. The Iranian regime is corrupt and violent, but they are not stupid, including that mad man, Ghorbani."

"When do I put to sea?"

"Exactly a week from today, in order to give our insiders time to listen in."

"So, it looks like I've got my orders, Mike. A pleasure to see you again."

———————————

"Wait, Ashley, I have some other things to tell you, some big things. I think you realize how much the President thinks of you, as well as your husband Jack. There's a reason why he promoted you to Fleet Admiral and Chairwoman of the Joint Chiefs of Staff. It's because you're the finest military officer in the country, as well as one of our best leaders, military or civilian."

Uh oh. High praise is always nice to be flattered with, but it usually accompanies a heavy message.

"As you know, the State of the Union Address is scheduled for the end of the week. I know from past experience that you and Jack like to attend the event, but on direct word from President Blake, I'm ordering you and Jack *not* to be there."

"But Mike, Jack and I love the State of the Union. We've been invited for the past six years, and we only missed it once because we were at sea. Why the snub?"

"It's not a snub, Ashley, it's a matter of national security. Take a deep breath because I'm about to blow your mind. You may be shocked to hear this, Ashley, but as of this afternoon you are on the list of *Designated Successors*, also known as *Designated Survivors*, which is usually limited to the Vice President, cabinet members, and high-ranking Senators. Yes, you heard me right.

In the event of a massive attack on the federal government, you, Ashley Patterson, are in line to become President of the United States. The President and Congress think that highly of you. That's why you can't attend the State of the Union— Protecting your life is of vital national concern."

Oh, my God, I'm in line to be President, far down the list, but nevertheless in line. Holy shit, I'm a *Designated Successor.* As Mike suggested, I took a deep breath.

"Ashley and Jack, it's been great seeing you folks, as always. The Chief of Naval Operations will be contacting you with the details of your upcoming deployment. Your only job for the State of the Union Address is *not* to be there. God bless you."

Yes, God bless us. Please, God, do just that. *Me,* a *Designated Successor* to the White House?

Chapter 31

Jack and I got into the staff car for our ride to the airport. Jack wrapped me in both arms and kissed me.

"Have I mentioned that I married well? Oh, my God, baby, you're in line to be President."

Whatever good happens to me, having Jack at my side always makes it better.

As we climbed the gangplank of the *Ford*, the officer of the deck announced, "Carrier Strike Group 3400, arriving." We saluted the flag and returned the salute of the OOD. Jack pulled me to the side and said, "Just think, honey, some day we may hear, 'United States of America, arriving.'

"Hey, Jack, I'm flattered by this honor, but the chance of me taking office is nil. I'm at the bottom of a long list of people."

"Yes, you're right, but nothing can take away the fact that you've been given a great honor. My God, you're a *Designated Successor*. You da girl, baby."

We walked into our quarters on the *Ford*. Jenny and Mike, my *Gang*, were waiting for us.

"Oh, my God almighty," Jenny shouted in her usual reserved

way. She hugged me. "Mike, show them the paper." Mike held up the latest issue of *Navy Times*. On the first page was a banner headline:

"United States Navy Admiral named to the list of 'Designated Successors' to become President of the United States in the event of a mass tragedy."

The article went on to discuss me and my background. I was happy to see that the article also talked about Jack. The *Navy Times* editors were obviously happy to see one of their own appointed to such a high position.

"Admiral Patterson is the youngest admiral in Navy history. President Blake recently named her a Fleet Admiral, the first since William Halsey, and shortly thereafter appointed her Chairwoman of the Joint Chiefs of Staff. The New York Times referred to her as 'The Navy's rising star.' She is the only military officer named a Designated Successor to the Presidency, which is usually limited to the Vice President, cabinet members, and Senators."

Mike popped the cork on a bottle of Moet Champagne. My *Wormhole Gang* was in a mood to celebrate. I love these people, but I felt a bit embarrassed at all the hoopla.

"Hey, you know how much I love you guys, but I think it's important that we all recognize something. I can't tell you how honored I am by this, but please keep in mind that for me to assume office, a hell of a lot of people must first die. Not a pleasant thought. As far as I'm concerned, this is nothing more than an honor, a high honor to be sure, but it's just an honor. There are a lot of terrific people ahead of me in line."

"But that's what we're celebrating tonight, Admiral Ashley, what an incredible honor it is for you to be named to this position," Jenny said. "I always think of you as my sister, and I can't be prouder. You're the best, Admiral."

"I love to party with my *Gang*, but I remind you that next week Carrier Strike Group 3400 casts off its lines and steams for the Persian Gulf. We have an important and scary deployment in front of us."

"With you running the show, Admiral Ashley, I'm not worried at all," Mike said.

Chapter 32

T oday is Thursday and we steam for the Persian Gulf on Monday. Jack, Jenny, and Mike, no surprise, had already handled the complicated details of deploying a Carrier Strike Group. My *Wormhole Gang* always gets the job done.

Tonight, President Blake will deliver the State of the Union Address before a Joint Session of Congress. So, it's time for yet another party at Jack's suggestion. Jack loves to party and whatever Jack loves, I'm all in. And we also love the State of the Union Address, whether on TV or preferably in person. It's like the Super Bowl of American politics. The Address has been delivered orally ever since Woodrow Wilson in 1913. It's carried on TV on every major network. It seems that everybody in the world will attend—except me and Jack. As a *Designated Successor*, it's my job to stay put, in accordance with tradition, custom, and national security. Me, a *Designated Successor*? Holy shit.

Jack and I always loved to attend the event, but orders are orders. I'd be lying if I didn't say I was flattered to take a knee tonight. Besides *The Gang*, we invited Captain Luke Barrett, Commanding Officer of the *Ford*, to join US, along with his wife Becky. The Barretts had just secured an apartment nearby, and Becky will stay there while Luke is deployed with CSG

3400. She's a freelance editor and is accustomed to working out of their living quarters. Luke had gotten over his bout with pneumonia, thank God.

Mike uncorked the champagne, and Luke unscrewed large bottles of scotch, vodka, and gin. *If the speech isn't good, at least we'll all get happily plastered.* Luke rose to propose a toast.

"To Ashley Patterson, the best damn admiral in the United States Navy and now a *Designated Successor* to the Presidency."

Luke is a good guy, a good friend, and a good captain. He also likes to flatter me.

At 9 p.m. Eastern Time, the address was scheduled to begin. We all sat, our eyes glued to the TV. *President Matt Blake is an excellent public speaker, one of the best in my opinion, so we all expected to be entertained, not just illuminated.* The room where the address will be given is huge, giving everyone a COVID-19-compliant six feet from the next person. For the first 10 minutes of the address, President Blake delivered the time-honored applause lines and then dove into the substance of his address.

"And now I'll discuss two gigantic problems facing our country, man-made time travel and Iran's violation of the nuclear arms agreement between the United States and Iran."

This was the part we'd all been waiting for, because it involves us—Man-made time travel and a possible nuclear war. I polished off my glass of vodka. We live in strange times, scary times, as President Blake just reminded us.

The TV suddenly went black. All our lights were still on, telling US we had no electricity problem. The on/off light showed that the TV was still on. *I wondered if our bookkeeper forgot to pay the cable TV bill.* Jack clicked from station to station on the remote. The minor stations that didn't carry the speech seemed to be working, but not the big networks. On one channel there was a show about the bear problems in the state parks. Next came a cooking show with tips on all the trimmings for a barbecue. Then came a show about the financial problems the Post Office had been going through. Finally, after about three minutes, *CBS* came on the air, with Norah O'Donnell reporting. Apparently, her job for the evening was to monitor the State of the Union from the *CBS* studio in New York and to provide commentary. Norah O'Donnell is well-known for her smooth, calm reporting of major events. She is a total pro and I'm a big fan of hers. I try to mimic her cool, steady delivery whenever I need to address the crew about something important over a ship or Strike Group PA system.

But the person we looked at was not the Norah O'Donnell we'd grown to know. She looked like she'd just fallen down a flight of stairs. She began by knocking over a water glass, soaking the papers in front of her. "Shit," she yelled as she mopped up the spill. Something's wrong. I couldn't believe Norah O'Donnell just yelled, yes *yelled*, the word *shit* in national TV. The bunch of us were speechless. There in front of us was the most unflappable TV reporter on any network looking scared out of her mind. She looked straight into the camera. Oh my God, now she was crying, her tears dragging the heavy TV makeup down her face. What the hell is going on?

"Ladies and gentlemen," she said, obviously trying to pull herself together, "I've just received word that a gigantic explosion has ripped through the Congressional Office Building as President Blake was delivering his State of the Union Address. Some observers think the blast may have been nuclear because it was so powerful."

She wiped some tears—and makeup—and continued

speaking, her voice halting.

"It's obvious, from a replay of the video, that any human being in that Congressional chamber has been killed, including...(*choke, sob*)...President Matt Blake, First Lady Dee, his cabinet, and all Senators and Members of the House of Representatives."

Dear God, our government has just been murdered.

The phone rang—and my life changed.

"It's former Senator Nancy Marsden for you, Admiral Ashley," Jenny whispered, clasping the phone to her chest. Tears ran down her face, having just heard about the death of her beloved cousin, President Blake.

Nancy Marsden, until her recent retirement, served as Senate Majority Leader. She is still known as one of Washington's heavyweights. Her current title is White House Spokesperson. Because of her duties at the White House, she didn't attend the State of the Union.

"Hello, Senator."

"Good evening, Madam President."

Chapter 33

G ood evening, ladies and gentleman, I'm Bret Baier, your *Special Report* host for *Fox News*. I'm about to deliver the most difficult news I've ever reported. Simply put, our government has been wiped out. As President Blake delivered the annual State of the Union Address, a powerful bomb exploded in the House Chamber of the United States Capitol building. Reports from the United States Army Corps of Engineers confirm that the bomb was a low-yield nuclear weapon.

"The entire Capitol building, that iconic symbol of American government, has been completely destroyed, along with any human being in the building. All members of the Senate, the House of Representatives, and the entire cabinet have been killed, along with President Blake, First Lady Dee, and the White House staff.

"It's a long-standing custom for certain cabinet members or Senators to miss the event in order to provide for a *Designated Successor,* also known as the grim words, *Designated Survivor.* In breaking with tradition, President Blake did not pick a cabinet member or Senator to skip the event, but instead selected the nation's senior military officer to be the *Designated Successor.*

"He chose the famous Ashley Patterson, Fleet Admiral and Chairwoman of the Joint Chiefs of Staff to be the *Designated Successor.* Admiral Patterson is now the President of the United States, the first woman to hold the office. She will be formally inaugurated, according to the 20th Amendment, on January 20, just under two weeks from now. But, by operation of law, she is now our President.

"Admiral Patterson is no stranger to critical events. She and her husband, Jack Thurber, spearheaded the United States' efforts to combat the nefarious man-made time travel plot, foisted by Iran. The word 'close' doesn't begin to describe the relationship between them. An article in *Time Magazine* once named them 'America's Lovebirds.' Jack Thurber, who I guess I should refer to as 'First Gentleman,' is the wealthy author and publisher, the CEO of Thurber Publishing Company. He often leaves his executive post to join his wife, Ashley, on one of her assignments. Jack Thurber holds the rank of captain in the Naval Reserve.

"It's not my position to editorialize, but I'm going to speak my mind, given the crisis facing our nation. We are fortunate to have a woman of courage, intelligence, and character lead us through this perilous time. Ashley Patterson is that woman.

"God bless you, President Patterson, and God bless us all.

"Bret Baier, signing off for *Fox News.*"

Chapter 34

W hat did you just call me, Senator?"

"I called you Madam President because that's who you are, the President of the United States."

"Wait a minute. Aren't you ahead of me on the list of succession?"

"I was until I retired last month. President Patterson, you're it. You may be at the bottom of the list of successors, but you're far from the bottom when it comes to talent and leadership skills. I pledge to you that I will do all in whatever power I have to help you in this difficult transition. In an incredible situation like this, you would normally expect a lot of phone calls, but I'm afraid you won't. Most of the would-be callers are dead."

Senator Marsden let go of a sob. "Our government has been wiped out, decimated, destroyed. You're the one, Madam President. As White House Spokesperson I've researched the protocols on what happens next. After clearing it through the Secret Service, and on their authority, I've taken the liberty of ordering Air Force One to pick up you and your husband at JFK tomorrow at 8 a.m. Supreme Court Justice Alex Rooney will meet you at the White House to swear you in, unless you choose a different location for the ceremony. I've also ordered a large Secret Service detail to guard your ship. Obviously, your inauguration can't be held at the Congressional Office Building, the customary location for the event, because the building has been totally destroyed. Judge Rooney is the only Justice who wasn't at the State of the Union because he's convalescing from an ankle fracture. As the new White House Spokesperson and most-recently-retired Senator, I will also be there for your swearing in, Madam President. God bless you. God bless all of us."

Jenny sat on the couch, crying her eyes out. She just found out that she lost her close friend and beloved cousin, President Matt Blake, along with his wife, First Lady Dee. I sat next to her and hugged her tightly. Mike was next to Jenny with his hand on her knee. Mixed emotions are something everybody deals with in life. Mine were beyond mixed, more like scrambled. It tore me to pieces to see my dear friend Jenny so upset. Mix that with my head spinning over hearing that I'm now the President of the United States. Me?

Jack, God bless him, walked over to the couch where I sat with Jenny. I stood and he hugged me. I needed a hug from Jack like never before. I looked into his eyes and he spoke to me in one of our wordless communications. His face told me he will never leave my side. That's exactly what I needed to know, with or without words.

I felt like I was about to pass out, and it wasn't from the vodka. Me, President of the United States? Oh my God.

Jenny rose and walked over to me, wiping tears from her eyes.

"Admiral Ashley, or I should say, Madam President, I'm going to do what President Matt would have wanted me to do, to pull my shit together and support you a thousand percent."

She returned my hug, sobbing as she did so.

Jack has an innate sense of knowing exactly what to do in any situation. He asked everyone to stand as he recited a prayer of condolence for all the lives lost from a prayer book that I keep with me, making special note of the loss of Jenny's cousin, President Blake. I will take that book with me to the White House. The White House? Holy shit.

"Let's hear your first speech as our Commander in Chief, Madam President," Jenny said after blowing her nose.

I took a healthy, maybe not so healthy, swig of vodka. Jenny just called me *Madam President*. I felt like I was on a different planet. I took a deep breath and began my first speech as POTUS. I didn't have a large audience, but it was the most important audience I could ever ask for.

"I think I speak for you guys as well as myself when I say that I'm stunned out of my mind. Our nation has just been turned upside down, and in a strange way of fate, the job has been dumped in my lap to put it right side up. After just hearing about the death of Jenny's cousin, President Blake, I realize that I have some big shoes to fill. You people have always been at my side, and now I will depend on you as never before. I'm experienced at skippering a ship or commanding a Carrier Strike Group. Hell, I'm a senior naval officer and I know what I'm doing. But of one thing I'm certain—I have absolutely no idea how to run a country. With your help and the help of a lot of people I don't even know, I'm going to get this job done. I won't let you guys down, and I ask you not to let *me* down. I love you all. God bless you. God bless all of us."

Chapter 35

Jack and I sat in Admiral's Quarters on the *Ford* and had an early breakfast. Jack detected that my mood was one of angst. Angst? I was scared out of my fucking mind.

"Here's what I suggest, honey. You're suddenly the head of a government that barely exists. You can't get it done all at once, so the only thing you can do is put one pretty foot forward and take it one step at a time."

"Jack, honey, I've just been given the highest command I could ever imagine. Although I'm an emotional wreck, I'm going to do what I always do when given an assignment, I'm going to get the job done. But I can't do it without you, baby. You have been my Chief of Staff for a long time and I want you to continue. The only difference is that you'll no longer be Chief of Staff to an admiral, but to the Commander in Chief. I cannot possibly handle this assignment without you by my side. You will also continue to hold your other positions—*my husband, my lover, and my best friend.*"

"Ash, honey, I'm flattered by your faith in me, but you know as well as I do that I have no idea how to run a government. My knowledge of politics and government matters is sketchy at best."

"Nonsense, baby. To run a government only requires two things—brains and courage, two words that accurately describe a man named Jack Thurber. The rest is all details, details that can be provided by people with actual knowledge. You, Jenny, and Mike are the beginnings of our new government. Last night I officially appointed them my Senior Aides. Now I need to call off our upcoming mission until I find a replacement commander for CSG 3400. I'm going to call CNO Jake Wayman."

I called Admiral Wayman and told him to think about a list of possible new COs of CSG 3400 to replace me. My hand was shaking. Jake is a tough guy, but I could tell he was crying as he congratulated me on becoming President. I felt strange to give orders to the Chief of Naval Operations, my former boss, but that's what it's going to be like going forward. Like it or not, I'm in charge. Wayman, like everyone else in the country, was stunned that we just lost our government, and for the time being, I'm it. I told Wayman to take whatever necessary steps to remove me and Jack from the ranks as Naval officers. Actually, as a Fleet Admiral, my position is permanent. How will that work? Do I formally retire? Two of the zillion questions I need answered. I also ordered him to continue as Chief of Naval Operations. Wayman promised to call me within the hour with his ideas for the next CO of CSG 3400. "Consider it done, Madam President."

"Jack, honey, we need to meet with *The Gang* and start to come up with a plan."

"I'll call Jenny and Mike now," Jack said.

Precisely one minute after Jack called, Jenny and Mike appeared in my office. Obviously, they'd been expecting Jack's call.

"Our new government begins right now," I said. "Jack, of course, is my Chief of Staff. Last night I officially appointed you two as my Senior Aides. You guys are going to help me pull all this shit together. You will both live in the White House, of course. You can decline this assignment, but I know you won't."

"Maybe Jenny and I should carry the official titles, *White House Wormhole Gangsters*," Mike said.

We all laughed. God, it felt good to laugh.

"So, I'll continue this meeting with an open question. What's next, guys?"

"*Who's* left is the big question?" Jenny said. "Last night we lost a lot of intelligent and talented people, most specifically my cousin, but they're not the only people who made this government work. None of us knows exactly who died last night, but we need to know who died and who's left." Jenny wiped more tears from her face when she mentioned her beloved cousin.

"Jenny, as usual, got it right," Jack said. "We need to get a list of those who attended the State of the Union—a list of dead people."

"I've got the list," Jenny said, no surprise. "It was in this morning's *New York Times* online. I printed out copies for all of us," She handed out copies of the article.

"Okay, nothing is more important than the four of us going through that list," I said. "Get set for some trauma. We're about to read a sickening obituary, a list full of dead people, many of whom each of us knew well, some as friends. Mike, I want you to make a list of who is alive, which is basically a list of names not in the *New York Times* article. Jenny, please read from the list starting from the top. If any of us thinks of a name, we'll just shout it out and Jenny will cross reference it.

"Buster," Jack said. Jenny looked at her list.

"Not on the list. He's alive, thank God," she said.

"Sarah Watson," I said, and bit my lip. Jenny said nothing. "Jenny, I said Sarah Watson."

Jenny put her face in her hands.

"She's on the list, Madam President. Sarah Watson is dead."

I couldn't help it, so I sobbed. I've always loved Sarah Watson, an outstanding FBI Director and a sweetheart of a human being. Now she's dead, murdered in cold blood as she sat listening to a speech.

"Okay, everybody, this isn't easy, but we've got to continue."

The list was in order by category. Jenny read off the names of the Joint Chiefs of Staff—*My* staff. All dead. I'd been in difficult meetings before, but this was the worst of my life. I once witnessed a horrible car accident involving five vehicles, two of which were open convertibles. Bodies were flung everywhere, none of them alive. Listening to Jenny read off those names made me think of that car accident. Sometimes the ugliness of life gets right in your face and refuses to go away.

Jenny then read off the names of all 435 members of the House of Representatives, followed by the 100 Senators. Our legislative branch of government. All dead, many of them my friends.

"We no longer have a government," I said, apropos of nothing, but yet apropos of everything.

Jack reached over and squeezed my hand.

"That's not quite accurate, baby. We *do* have a government— and you're it."

Jenny then read the category of past presidents who were in attendance. One name was missing, which meant that one former president survived: George H. Conklin.

"But why would George Conklin miss the State of the Union?" I said. "I've had the pleasure of meeting him, and he's always willing to lend his face to important historical events."

Mike grabbed the newspaper and rifled through it, going from article to article. I've always been impressed at how Mike speed reads.

"Here it is," Mike said, "a short article on page six. The title of the article reads, *Former President George H. Conklin unable to attend the State of the Union because of a bout with the COVID-19 virus. He's expected to fully recover.*

"Thank God, Conklin is alive," I said. "More than anybody he can help me figure out what to do. He was always ready to step up to the bat with foreign policy, and he was never afraid to flex military muscle. I've always liked the guy, and I think he's somebody I can talk to. And we're both members of the same political party, The Freedom Party. I'm going to call him now. That article said he's expected to recover, so hopefully he can talk to me."

Jenny, God bless her, realized right away that I will need a Rolodex the size of an encyclopedia. She has a mind like a file cabinet, and knows just how to find phone numbers, even unlisted ones.

Jenny gave me his phone number and I called him at his home in Philadelphia.

"The Conklin residence, Maggie Blackwell speaking. How may I help you?"

Shit, I just realized that I hadn't come up with a way to introduce myself on the phone. Well, simply telling the truth usually does the trick.

"This is President Patterson, may I please speak to President Conklin?"

"Oh, my God, Madam President. President Conklin is still a bit under the weather, but I'm sure he'll want to speak to you. Congratulations, by the way. After our incredible national tragedy, at least we have a new President we can count on. I'm his aide, by the way. Feel free to phone me at any time, Madam President, and please call me Maggie. My dad was a Navy captain and we both followed the stories about you. I'm a big fan of yours."

Nice to know I have a fan club. I'll need it.

"President Patterson, what a delight to hear from you," President Conklin said after he coughed. "After the horror of last night, at least our country has you as a wonderful new leader. I hate being sick, but my little case of COVID-19 saved my life. I'm glad I didn't listen to people who told me to wear a face mask. My procrastination saved my life. Please call me George."

"I hope you're feeling better, George, and please call me Ashley. Yesterday was the most shocking day of my life. First, I found out that I was a *Designated Successor,* and then discovered that my designation became the real thing. The alternate name for *Designated Successor* is *Designated Survivor.* Looks like I'm it. At the risk of overstating the obvious, George, I need to put together a government. Thank God that we're both members of the Freedom Party. We'll be working together a lot if that's okay with you. You will be a big help in putting together my cabinet. We also need conventions of the Freedom Party and the America First Party to run slates of candidates for future Senators and members of the house."

"Do you know the party leaders, Ashley?"

"Hey, George, for the past few years I've spent most of my time at sea. I don't even know who those people are."

"Well, thank God, they're both still alive, neither of them having attended the State of the Union. The head of our party, the Freedom Party, is Sam Tomkins, and the leader of the America First Party is Mildred Frank, better known as Millie. Although she will be your opposition, she's an easy person to get along with and she isn't hesitant to cross the aisle and work for a common goal. I'd volunteer to reach out to them, Ashley, but I suggest that you ask your husband, Jack, to do so. I know well how close you two are, and I have no doubt that he is your Chief of Staff, whether or not he officially carries the title. His name needs to be out there in public, especially among political leaders. Maggie will email their telephone numbers as we talk if you give us your contact information. I don't doubt for an instant that they will be calling you. I have taken the liberty of calling Tim Boyle, Deputy Director of the Secret Service, whose job was to miss the State of the Union. His boss, Secret Service Chief Pete French, is dead. A large Secret Service detail is already stationed next to your ship, thanks to a call from White House Spokeswoman, former Senator Nancy Marsden. Tim himself will escort you and Jack to your new home."

"My new home?"

"Yes, Ashley, the White House."

"The White House? Holy shit, of course."

Now that I'm President of the United States, I really should watch my salty language. Fuck it, my life has just changed forever.

"It will take me a few days to shake the virus, Ashley, but we'll be in touch by phone. I've already put together a proposed list of cabinet members for you to look at. Good night, Madam President. We'll talk tomorrow."

Former President Conklin just called me *Madam President?* This is going to take some getting used to.

Chapter 36

The Wormhole Gang continued our meeting after I got off the phone with President Conklin. No surprise, the three of them were an explosion of ideas and suggestions. My *Gang* never lets me down. The phone rang again, and Jenny picked up.

"President Patterson's Office, may I help you?" Jenny was stepping right into her role as the President's Aide.

"Yes, sir, she's right here. It's Tim Boyle of the Secret Service for you, Madam President."

"Hello, Madam President, I'm at the gangplank of the *Ford* and I request permission to come aboard."

"Come on up, Tim." I've decided to call people by their first names. Is that appropriate? I really don't know. I guess I'll adjust to this stuff—eventually.

Tim Boyle, the new Director of the United States Secret Service, was piped aboard. His title was not announced by the OOD as it normally is. Nobody heard an announcement that said, "Secret Service, arriving." Secret means *secret.*

Tim Boyle is a tall, handsome black man at 6'4." His bearing announced, "Don't give me any shit and I won't give any to you." He has an engaging personality that makes you want him as a friend. But he'll more than my friend. His job is to keep me alive. *Ouch.* Mike met him on the quarterdeck and escorted him to my office.

"Madam President, it's an honor to meet you. Hello, Captain Thurber. As you know, the ship is surrounded by a large Secret Service detail. It's now time, but of course it's up to you, to move you and your belongings to your new home, the White House. A fleet of SUVs awaits you."

Oh my God. These guys are moving us to the White House. The White Friggin House!

"Are you okay, Ma'am?"

"Yes, I didn't get much sleep last night." How about none.

"My research tells me that you will want to have your *Wormhole Gang* with you, Jennifer Blake and Michael Jackson. I've arranged for quarters for them at the White House."

He turned to Jenny. "Ms. Blake, your cousin, the late President Blake, told me all about you and your husband. He was quite fond of you two, to say the least. I'm honored to meet you, and I'm sorry for your loss."

Tim Boyle, whose job is to kick ass occasionally, couldn't have been more of a gentleman, and we all appreciated it. I also appreciated the bulge of a pistol under his jacket.

Captain Luke Barrett, CO of the *Ford*, joined us as we were packing to move. Although I hadn't told the Chief of Naval Operations yet, Captain Luke is my pick as Commanding Officer of Carrier Strike Group 3400. I'll also be promoting him to rear admiral.

"Admiral, or I should say, Madam President, I can't tell you what an honor it's been to serve with you and Captain Jack. I will never forget the little party last night that you and Jack hosted as we watched the State of the Union address. Our world suddenly changed. The only positive thing about our upsetting gathering is that we learned that Ashley Patterson is the new President of the United States. Our country is fortunate to be in good hands."

Captain Luke then saluted me and broke down in tears. I don't think of him as a subordinate, but more like a friend. I couldn't wait to tell him about his promotion and new command, so I didn't. I hadn't yet cleared it with the CNO, but screw it, I'm the boss.

"Luke, I hereby promote you to rear admiral and assign you to command Carrier Strike Group 3400." Totally against protocol, he hugged me. His eyes looked like saucers when I addressed him as Admiral.

The Secret Service guys aren't just security people, they're energetic as hell. Six of them humped the belongings of the *Wormhole Gang* to the waiting SUVs.

As the four of us descended the gangplank of the *Ford* for the last time, the officer of the deck announced, "United States of America, departing." Oh my God. This was the first time I'd been officially acknowledged as the holder of my new office. After saluting OOD and the flag, I filled up, tears running down my face. I really need to knock off this emotional crap. I looked at Jack, who was also teary eyed. As long as Jack is at my side, nothing's wrong with strong emotions. I've shed more tears in the past 24 hours than I've shed in my entire life. But with Jack by my side, I have no reason to cry.

Jack, Jenny, Mike, and I sat in the huge SUV limo. The interior was spacious enough so we were able to keep six feet from each other. This had nothing to do with "social distancing"—hell we're family—It had to do with working the phones.

We have a government to put together.

The SUV drove us to JFK airport where Air Force One awaited us. Oh my God, *Air Force One*. I felt like I was dreaming. I now have my own private means of transportation—Air Force Friggin One. I need a drink.

Chapter 37

When we arrived at JFK our driver brought us directly to Air Force One. I took a deep breath as I read the words on the fuselage of the huge 747: "United States of America." My heart, as usual, was pounding. At 1445 we pulled up to the West Wing of the White House. Make that 2:45 p.m. I should really learn to talk like a civilian. *Roger that, over.*

Today is Monday, January 4. Although I've been sworn in already, I'm about to take the oath of office as President. I will be officially inaugurated on January 20, as per the 20th Amendment to the United States Constitution. Because of COVID-19, it will be a small ceremony. In consultation with Jack, former Senator Nancy Marsden, and former President Conklin, I chose retired four-star General Wayne Summers to serve as my Vice President. I drilled them on whether picking another military officer is a good idea, and we all agreed that the world situation called for military experience at the top. General Wayne had once served on the Joint Chiefs of Staff as Army Chief of Staff. As Chairwoman of the Joint Chiefs, I was once his boss, and he impressed the hell out of me. Looks like I'm his boss once again. Fortunately, he retired a week before the State of the Union, just missing being killed. Wayne is a good guy, smart as a whip, with a great sense of humor. His wife,

Gayle Summers, is a terrific lady. Like her husband, Gayle is smart, and shares Wayne's affection for cracking jokes. Gayle is a West Point graduate and met her future husband when they were fellow cadets. She decided not to pursue a military career and mustered out of the Army as a captain. She is a professor of history at American University. I've always hated the idea of a President keeping the VP in the dark about pending matters. That won't happen with Wayne and me. I was happy to see that he and Jack hit it off like old pals. Gayle and I get along great too. "I was a West Point cadet during the same time you were a midshipman at Annapolis, Madam President. For four years we kicked your ass every year at the Army-Navy Game." Definitely an easy lady to get along with.

Any time I've been to the White House on official business I always felt like hot shit. Now I'm here as President of the United States. That counts as hot shit, I guess. We were escorted to the second floor of the West Wing, the personal living quarters of the first family. It is both opulent, and somewhat understated. I could tell that Mr. Moneybags Jack was already redesigning the place. I reminded him that the money in question belongs to the American taxpayers. Jack mentioned that he's willing to use his own money, of which he has plenty. We'll see.

During our flight, I skimmed through a book about the memoirs of former Presidents. Jenny, no surprise, had found the book for me. It was clear that all Presidents felt a sense of overwhelm on the day they moved in. With me it was no different, but maybe even more so. I never ran for this office, and frankly, never even thought about it. I'm a *Designated Successor,* also known as a *Designated Survivor,* and took this job as a result of a national tragedy. But I *did* accept the job and I'm determined to give this assignment my best as I always do. Jack agrees. I don't know a hell of a lot about politics, but I do know a thing or two about leadership. I decided to put my self-doubt on permanent hold. It has no place in the Oval Office.

After Tim Boyle and his Secret Service guys left, Jack walked over and hugged me. Jack has an innate sense of knowing what I need. And I definitely needed a hug. As he held me, I buried my face in his neck and stroked my hands along his muscular back. This wonderful man will make my new job doable.

After we "moved in," I sat behind my desk in the Oval Office, not quite believing it was me. My desk is known as the Resolute Desk, a gift from Queen Victoria to President Rutherford B. Hayes in 1880. It was built from the oak timbers of the British exploration ship *HMS Resolute*. Talk about history!

As I sat at my Resolute Desk, I contemplated that most commentators consider me the most powerful person in the world. Holy shit. Me?

Jack insisted that I enter the Oval Office by myself. He's committed to the idea that I needed to jump right into the job on my own. So, I did, but no way could I handle this position without Jack. As we planned, he joined me a few minutes later. We sat in two armchairs at the end of the two sofas facing the Resolute Desk. I refused to have Jack sit in front of my desk. Hey, he's Jack. *My Jack.*

By tradition, each new President gets to redesign the office for personal preference. But I had bigger things to do than furniture arrangement. I needed to form a government.

At 1530 (3:30 p.m.), Buster showed up for our planned meeting. Reappointing Buster as CIA Director was one of my first official acts and it was a no-brainer. I can do worse than having a super spook as the nation's top spy. I also invited General Wayne Summers, my Vice-Presidential pick. We sat on the facing couches, Buster on one side next to General Summers, Jack and me on the other.

"Madam President," Buster said, "I know I've said this before in our brief phone conversation, but our country is damn lucky to have a leader like you running the show. You're the best, Ashley, I mean Madam President. And you've picked an excellent Vice President, General Summers here."

"Thanks for your kind words, Buster. I just hope I won't give you a reason to hurl cusswords at me. So, there are two things we need to talk about, both of which involve Iran: the man-made wormhole program and the violations of the nuclear arms agreement. Anything else, Buster?"

"Yes, there is, Madam President—the bombing of the State of the Union Address. My inside guys in Tehran suspect that the bombing was ordered by Prime Minister Ghorbani. They aren't certain, but they have strong suspicions."

"Once we have conclusive evidence, I'm prepared to declare war on Iran. Two things concern me: I haven't gone through the official inauguration yet, and we don't have a Congress in place to ratify my decisions. But I've already taken the oath of office and the official inauguration will be in two weeks, so that takes care of problem number one. We can have a Congressional election in two months. If Iran pulls off any more shit, I'm ready to declare war as an executive decision. Lousy way to start an administration, but no fucking way will I allow an unanswered attack on our country."

I really need to watch my foul mouth.

"When President Blake appointed you as a *Designated Successor*," Jack said, "he sure didn't pick a pussy cat."

"Okay, guys, we've gone as far as we can for now. Keep the safeties off on your firearms."

Chapter 38

Today is January 20, the day of my official inauguration as President of the United States. Because I couldn't be sworn in at the Capitol Building which had been destroyed, I chose the steps of the Supreme Court building. Jack and I, along with Jenny and Mike, piled into *The Beast*, the biggest bad-ass SUV I'd ever seen—my official Presidential limo. *The Beast* was tricked out to withstand a bomb attack and it gets the gas mileage of an army tank.

At 29 degrees with a stiff wind, it was cold as the Arctic. Supreme Court Justice Alex Rooney awaited us, freezing his ass off even though he wore a heavy topcoat. He still wore a cast on his right leg from his ankle fracture after playing tennis. That lucky fracture saved his life, causing him to skip the mass murder scene at the State of the Union Address. He gave me a bright smile even though his lips shivered. Responding to his request, I placed my right hand on the Bible. Oh my God, I'm about to be formally sworn in as President of the United States.

"I do solemnly swear that I will faithfully execute the Office of President of the United States, and will to the best of my ability, preserve, protect, and defend the Constitution of the

United States."

So that was it. I'm now officially the POTUS, although I technically assumed office the moment President Blake died. Maybe my heart will stop pounding. Maybe not.

Jenny reminded me that President William Henry Harrison died of pneumonia in 1841, 32 days after his swearing in. It was her polite way of reminding me to keep my acceptance speech short. Every time she opens her mouth, Jenny shows why I picked her as my Chief Aide. Why the hell can't Inauguration Day be a week after the election in early November? Why not May or June? Poor President Harrison would have liked that. Okay, time for my (short) speech.

"My fellow Americans. I stand before you as the newly inaugurated President of the United States. I am acutely aware that you didn't elect me, and I take this office as a *Designated Successor* to President Blake. I serve by statute, not by an election. That said, you have my solemn promise that I will serve this office as if you wanted me to be here, not by the whims of tragedy. We may keep socially distant because of the COVID pandemic, but we are not distant from our love of this great country."

I could see that everybody was shivering as the wind suddenly picked up. Time to cut it short.

"I won't let you down, my fellow Americans. God bless you, and God bless the United States of America."

They applauded like crazy. Everybody wore face masks because of COVID-19. Although some people find face masks annoying, I think they were happy to keep their noses warm. I think they were also pleased that I kept my speech short and were clapping to keep their hands warm. The *Wormhole Gang* climbed into *The Beast* for the short drive to the White House. The Secret Service driver, God bless him, had run the engine to warm it up.

Time for a top-level meeting. I guess my days of bottom or mid-level meetings are over. I've taken quite a liking to retired Senator Nancy Marsden. She's a sharp lawyer, according to Jenny's research, and was once the Chairwoman of the Senate Judiciary Committee. She was also on the list of *Designated Successors,* and a fellow member of the Freedom Party. I asked her to be White House Counsel and I was delighted that she accepted. Nancy is not only a proven leader, she also has a sweet personality and is easy to get along with. Working closely with people who aren't on big ego trips is a priority with me. I thought about hanging a sign on the Oval Office door that said, "Caution—This is a No-Bullshit Zone." Jack didn't think it was a good idea. He's probably right.

Also at the meeting was Buster from the CIA, Sam Tomkins, head of the Freedom Party, and Millie Frank, Chairwoman of the America First Party. I invited Past President Conklin, but he's home getting over the last few days of the COVID-19 virus. The *Wormhole Gang,* Jack, Jenny, and Mike were there. As my Chief of Staff, Jack was chairman of the meeting.

First on the agenda were the soon-to-be-held conventions of the country's two major political parties, the Freedom Party and the America First Party. I made it clear to Sam Tomkins and Millie Frank, the party leaders, that I would not publicly support any candidates. I don't have any visceral distaste for politics, but in my unique position as *Designated Successor,* I strongly felt that I shouldn't be involved in partisan politics in the first go-around. Later, of course, but not now. Some people will hate me, I'm sure, but I don't want to give them a reason just yet. That will come soon enough when I make my Supreme Court picks, which will be shortly. Sam and Millie decided to hold their nominating conventions a week apart, the Freedom Party going first on February 3. The runoff election is scheduled for March, a change from normal scheduling because of the mass-tragedy. Soon, we'll have a complete government.

My next immediate job is to replace the eight dead Supreme Court justices. I asked Nancy Marsden, my White House Counsel, for recommendations. I also asked for input from the deans of Harvard, Stamford, Yale, and the University of Chicago, all recommended by Nancy. As White House Counsel, Nancy lined up the recommendations. I also asked for suggestions from Admiral Randolph Stone, an old friend of mine who once headed up the Navy Judge Advocate General Corps. I made them all aware of my judicial philosophy, even though I'm not a legal scholar. I want to appoint strict constructionists, people who see themselves as judges who interpret the Constitution as written, not some clowns who see the Court as a sort of alternate legislature consisting of nine unelected lawyers. Nancy Marsden shares my views.

After our meeting, Jack and I decided to take a walk around the grounds to let off steam. We were accompanied, of course, by a detail of Secret Service agents. The temperature had warmed up to a tolerable 45 degrees. We both felt good. After one long meeting, we had set the outline for a new American government. This is a lot more complicated than naval warfare.

Chapter 39

Ahmad Rafshandi here.

I don't know whether to feel proud or frightened. I've taken the gigantic step of switching sides and I've allied myself with the Americans (unofficially, of course). I definitely feel patriotic, putting myself in secret opposition to that insane madman, Prime Minister Ghorbani, who risks the destruction of Iran. I've done the right thing for my country.

The structure of the American government has been destroyed by a low-yield nuclear bomb. Although he hasn't admitted it, I believe that Prime Minister Ghorbani is behind the attack. I'm about to meet with him, and I already know what he wants to talk about. He'll want to know why I didn't brief him about the new American President. I didn't brief him because I had no idea who the *Designated Successor* was until the announcement after the bombing. Typical of the Americans, they, or rather he, President Blake, chose an outstanding and courageous military leader, Admiral Ashley Patterson. Her job, as the *Designated Successor,* is to step in and seamlessly continue the executive branch of the United States government. Admiral Patterson is, as the Americans would say, "tough as nails," even though she's a beautiful, sexy woman. I admire her as much as I despise my prime minister, especially because she is not one to put up with the bullshit of my esteemed leader. Things are about to get interesting.

According to my top-secret agreement with Buster, Director of the CIA, I pass information on to my wife, Donia, who then relays it to her sister Yasamin, who is married to top CIA agent, Max Hart. If I'm caught, I hope they'll kill me quickly, not torture me to death as the Prime Minister is fond of doing.

"I hope you are prepared to explain." Ahmad, "why you didn't alert me about the new American President. That heathen bitch, Ashley Patterson, has long been a thorn in my side, first as a naval warrior, and now as the political leader of the United States. She has interfered with my plans before, and now she is in a position to thwart them. I will not allow that to happen. So, tell me, Ahmad, how did this go beyond our understanding?"

"Your Excellency, the Americans have a procedure for continuing the government in the event of a major catastrophe, such as the bombing of the State of the Union Address. The procedure is known as a *Designated Successor*, also known as the *Designated Survivor*. A person is chosen to be absent from major events like the State of the Union in order to take control of the government immediately. For security reasons, the identity of the *Designated Successor* is kept secret until it's announced. There is no way I could have known it was Admiral Patterson until it was announced publicly. If I knew the bombing was about to occur, I could have made inquiries, but, of course, I had no idea about the bombing, or who ordered it."

Oh my God, what did I just do? I just raised a question about something I should have known nothing about—the bombing of the American government. My life is now on the line. What else is new?

"Of course, I ordered the bombing, Ahmad. Do you think for a minute that I wouldn't take advantage of a gathering of almost the entire American government? I expect that you should be aware of American plans without you knowing our secrets. I expect more of you, Ahmad. I now order you to keep me advised about President Patterson's intentions. I don't trust that bitch, and I demand to know inside information."

He slammed his hand on the desk, causing his cat to scurry to his usual hiding place under the sofa.

"Yes, Your Excellency, I will get right on the matter immediately."

Oh, dear Lord, I now possess the most explosive information imaginable. Yes, it was Iran that wiped out the entire American government. I need to act before I'm assassinated.

Chapter 40

Buster is on line one, Madam President. He sounds excited about something and wants to see you," Jenny said. Jenny had seamlessly taken on her job as my Chief Aide.

"Madam President, I have some earth-shaking news. May I see you immediately?"

I agreed to see him immediately, of course. Buster, the cool, calm spook, sounded like he was about to explode. I was sitting in the Oval Office with Jack. He would stay for my meeting with Buster. There is nothing I can hear that Jack cannot, and Buster is well aware of that. Jack loves to say that sometimes he and I disappear and reappear as one person. That will continue in the Oval Office.

Jenny showed him in.

"Hello, Madam President, hello Jack. Well, our big question has been answered. It was Iran that bombed the State of the Union Address. Our new inside contact, Ahmad Rafshandi, just communicated the word to CIA Agent Hart and I contacted him to confirm the information. I know that you're up to your eyeballs forming a new government, but I felt that couldn't wait to drop this news on you."

"As you're well aware, Buster, if I declare war, I want it to be clean as a whistle, which includes Congressional ratification. Problem is, we don't yet have a Congress. A Congressional runoff election will be held in March. As I've said many times, if an attack is imminent, I'll pull the trigger, but not until then. Did this Rafshandi guy give you any further information?"

"Yes, Ma'am, he did. Rafshandi thinks that that Prime Minister Ghorbani is out of his mind, a 'fucking lunatic,' according to him. Ghorbani is especially upset that you are our new President. According to Rafshandi, Ghorbani hates the fact that you're a woman. He thinks you should be in the kitchen, not in a leadership position."

"He's never tasted her cooking," wise guy Jack commented, resulting in my smack to his arm.

After he stopped laughing Buster said. "My big concern, Madam President, is that Ghorbani may be training his sights on the White House. In a matter of minutes, he destroyed our former government. Could the new Executive Branch, meaning you, be next? Jack, I recommend that you double up on Secret Service manpower. Well, I've done enough to screw up your day, so I'll be shoving off. I'll let you know immediately if I hear anything else."

Jack and I sat there having one of our wordless conversations. The White House, meaning me, is in Ghorbani's crosshairs. Jack too.

"The Greenbrier," we both said. It's a common occurrence when Jack and I share the same simultaneous thought. We often joke with each other that it's like a simultaneous climax.

"Hey, that's not a bad idea," I said. "The new Capitol office building won't be ready for well over a year, and the Greenbrier was once set up to House Congress and the Executive Branch when the place was chosen as an emergency location of government in case of a disaster. And we sure as hell have had a disaster. According to both Bill and Zeke Wellfleet, they have a well-armed military. It can be supplemented with our Army and Marine Corps."

"Ashley, hon, I think this is an idea whose time has come. I've always thought West Virginia was a better seat of government than Washington, and I know you think so too. It's a hell of a lot safer. Knowing how fast those *Keepers of Time* people move, we can be good to go within weeks. I think the Wellfleet boys will love the idea. Obviously, we'll pay them a good slug of rent because we'll basically be taking over the resort."

"Jack, baby, as soon as I clear this with the Wellfleets, please contact the party leaders and let them know the Congress they're about to elect will have a new mailing address."

"What if they don't like the idea?"

"Jack, honey, *tell* them, don't ask them. This is my order, not my opinion, and I don't give a rat's ass if they have a problem with it." "You are one tough broad, Madam President, I mean, Sweetheart."

Chapter 41

A date keeps flashing before my mind—April 13, 2022, two months from now. As we learned on our time travel into the future, that is the date when Iran will launch a nuclear war, plunging the world into darkness and chaos. That is the date the world as we know it will end. All of the other zillion decisions I've had to make are at the bottom of my list compared to April 13. It's time to act.

Jack walked into the Oval Office, followed by VP Wayne, Jenny and Mike. So, my *Wormhole Gang* was there, including our newest member, VP Wayne. We reviewed for Wayne the horrors we saw when we time travelled to New York City and saw a post-nuclear wasteland. We also went over what Bill Wellfleet told us about the lead up to the war and its barbaric aftermath. Wayne, a tough-as-nails retired General, sat there looking stupefied. Wayne had heard this before, but not in the detail we just gave him.

"As you ordered, Madam President, I've contacted every member of Congress, both the Senate and the House, and they confirmed what they already told you. If you declare war on Iran, your decision will be backed up by Congress. You and Jack were wise to tell them what you just told me—the impending nuclear war and the end of western civilization. Congress is on your side, Ma'am."

"Wayne, I want your opinion as a former General and Army Chief of Staff."

"I recommend that we pull the trigger, Madam President. As we all know, Iran's Prime Minister, Ahura Ghorbani, is not a rational human being. There's no negotiating with him. I don't doubt for a minute that he sees April 13 as his beloved 'End of Days.' I don't think we have any choice but to stop him. Madam President, you and I are former military people, and we know that war can be horrible, but I don't think we have much of a choice."

Jenny and Mike sat there silent. They looked uncomfortable, to say the least. But I see my fellow *Wormhole Gangsters* as two of the sharpest people I've ever met. They both have future leadership roles in our country, and I had no hesitation to bring them in on this high-level discussion. But I understood their desire to listen and not talk.

"Jack, what are your thoughts?"

"I think an attack may not be necessary."

The room went completely silent. This was the last thing I expected to hear.

"Jack, honey, please explain."

"I spoke to Buster just a few minutes ago. He told me that a few of his people are going to 'have a *talk*' with Ghorbani and his people today. We all know what that means."

Chapter 42

Bret Baier for *Fox News,* ladies and gentlemen. I have a major breaking story to report. There has been a violent coup in Tehran. We have it from confirmed sources that Iranian Prime Minister Ghorbani has been assassinated, along with members of his staff. Farhad Ahmadi, Iran's Foreign Minister, has taken over the reins of power. Here is a video clip, taken moments ago, of a scene on the street in front of the Prime Minister's office.

"As you can see, the huge crowd can best be described as jubilant. As we've known for months, the late Prime Minister Ghorbani was extremely unpopular with the citizens of Iran, and the scene we're looking at seems to confirm that.

"I have with us on the line, Arthur McDevitt, United States Secretary of State. Please give us the opinion of the State Department on this shocking development, Mr. Secretary."

"Although we never condone violence in politics, this event is not without some positive aspects. Foreign Minister Ahmadi, who is now Prime Minister, is well known for his intelligence and moderation. I was pleased to see that he has announced that an election will be held next month to confirm his position in office. I have an appointment to meet with him tomorrow in Tehran. Thank you for inviting me on your show, Bret. I'll be happy to return and give your viewers further details on this amazing development."

"Stay tuned *to Fox News* for the latest updates on this momentous story. Bret Baier signing off for *Fox News.*"

Chapter 43

Jenny did a cartwheel as Mike unlocked the liquor cabinet.

"So, it appears that Buster's boys did, indeed 'have a talk' with Ghorbani's people," I said.

"Madam President, the CIA Director is here," one of my assistants said. "I don't have him down as having an appointment."

"Show him right in, Mary."

Jenny, who knows Buster well, handed him a scotch on the rocks. Jack and Buster bear hugged.

"Buster, of course you had nothing to do with today's big news," I said, winking, "but fill us in on what you know."

"That's right, Madam President, I had nothing to do with it. I just watch the news like everybody else." With a big smile on his face, he chuckled as he said that. Buster's agents 'having talks' with people is one of the CIA's biggest secrets. Even though I'm Commander in Chief, I never ask for details on Buster's 'talks.' My need to know isn't for the public to know.

"So, fill us in on Iran's new government. Dear Lord, it appears that we won't need to go to war."

"No, Ma'am, war is now off the table, thank God. I know that you and Jack are aware of my relationship with Farhad Ahmadi as well as Hashem Mohammadi, his former deputy when he was foreign minister. They're good people, Madam President, and I consider them friends. We were in regular contact prior to the coup. They both went to college in the United States, and think of America as a friend, not *The Great Satan*. Ahmadi himself called me this morning to let me know that their nukes are in lock down, and on his order the wormhole-creating satellites have been disabled. We've just lost an enemy and gained a friend."

"So, it's safe to say that *The Wormhole Crisis* is no longer a crisis."

"That's right, Madam President. One less thing on your busy desk."

Chapter 44

The Iranian coup d'état was the best thing that happened to my presidency so far. The world is rid of those insane bastards in Tehran, and now we have a friend and ally in what was once a dangerous enemy.

I called Zeke Wellfleet at the Greenbrier to tell him about our idea of relocating the government to his resort.

"Oh, my God, Ashley, I mean Madam President, we're honored beyond belief," Zeke said. "The idea of the Greenbrier being the seat of our government is beyond my dreams. Hell, until the plan was abandoned, the Greenbrier was the alternate seat of the American government. I know Bill will love the idea too."

"Zeke, the idea makes a lot of sense to us, especially because the Greenbrier was once designed as the seat of the American government. As you probably know we will soon have 435 Congress people, 100 Senators, as well as aides and support staff. The runoff election will be held in March. The Executive Branch is huge with 15 Departments, most of whom can remain in Washington, with the Department heads and staff at the Greenbrier. Figure about 2,000 people for the top of the Executive Branch. Because we'll essentially be taking over the place, you will be compensated accordingly. How long do you think it will take to prepare the place?"

"We never changed the layout drastically after the relocation plan was dropped. We can use some help to whip it into shape. If the government can spare about 100 construction people to help, maybe from the U.S. Army Corps of Engineers, the Greenbrier can be ready to be the new seat of government in less than a month. My wife, Bobbie, is listening in on speaker and she's going nuts over the idea."

"What a fabulous plan, Madam President," Bobbie said, actually shouted. "The Greenbrier and the *The Keepers of Time* will be honored. Holy shit, pardon my West Virginia language, I can't wait for this to happen."

"And I've got good news about the COVID-19 pandemic," I said. "A vaccine should be ready in a week. Tests have shown it to be 95 percent effective. So, you folks won't need to worry about hundreds of government people infecting your lovely Greenbrier."

"And that coup d'état in Iran also seems to be great news," Zeke said.

———

I asked Jack, who else, to manage the enormous task of relocating the government to West Virginia. Typical of him, Jack thought the job sounded like a lot of fun. Fun? That's my Jack. He'd think slipping on ice and falling on his ass is fun. He asked me to assign Vice President Summers to help him manage the project, and I agreed. Summers has a reputation for getting things done, and he and Jack get along like old buddies.

The idea of running a government from a luxury resort

sounds weird when you think about it. But ever since I took over as *Designated Successor* everything is weird. We'll make this work. With Jack as honcho of the project I have no doubt about it. With all the shit piled on my desk, I keep my head screwed on by daydreaming about our fantasy of owning a bed and breakfast in the sticks. Now all I need is a government.

Chapter 45

Four Months Later

Today is March 3, 2021. Yesterday was Election Day, and the government no longer consists of just me, but I'm still the only unelected official. All the results are in. Although a few of the House elections were close, nobody has chosen to contest the election. It seemed that everybody, including career politicians, just wanted to move on, to get back to normal, whatever *normal* is. So, we have a government, thank God.

The Freedom Party, my party, controls the Executive Branch, of course, and holds a five-seat majority in the Senate. The America First Party has a six-member majority in the House. My Senate majority means that all my Supreme Court picks will be seated. This will result in a large hue and cry by the press and the opposition party. Tough shit. Numbers are numbers, and these numbers happen to work in my favor.

The White House could change its name to the Secret Service House. The place crawled with agents. Buster's concern about the White House, meaning me, becoming the next target resulted in security like a war zone. Even so, I felt a lot safer on the bridge of an aircraft carrier.

Our plans to move the government to the Greenbrier is going well, thanks to Jack and Vice President Summers. I visited the Greenbrier last week to check out our plans. I was happy to see the place fortified like an Army base. I think Jack and I had a good idea to locate the government there. As the *Designated Survivor*, I want to keep my status as a *survivor*.

Tonight, I will welcome our newly elected legislature at a Joint Session of Congress. Because there was no more Capitol Building and the Greenbrier isn't ready yet, we chose the large Lauinger Library at Georgetown University. The security made the place look like a war zone.

I kept my speech nonpartisan as I had planned. My status as *Designated Successor* screamed for that approach. *Kick Ass Ashley* will take command later, but for now it's *Make Nice Ashley*.

Judging from the applause from both sides of the aisle, my speech was well-received. We'll see how long that lasts. My combat experience is a good background for electoral politics.

Chapter 46

The Royal Caribbean ship, *Majesty of the Seas*, cast off her lines from her dock on the West Side of Manhattan, her destination Bermuda. It was the final cruise for Captain James Gordon before his retirement. He had just purchased a 65-foot yacht and looked forward to his second career as a charter boat captain. He stood on the bridge with Tim Wellington, his First Officer.

"I think the government has finally gotten a handle on that goddam wormhole problem, Tim. I haven't heard any news reports about the problem in over a month. Imagine steaming along and all of a sudden you slip into a different dimension of time. Another thing that gives me confidence is that only one ship that slipped through a wormhole was commercial. All the others were Navy ships. I'm looking forward to retiring—in the present time, please God."

"I don't feel as positive as you do, Skipper. The government announced that they *think* they destroyed the main wormhole-creating satellite, but they haven't offered any scientific facts, just opinions. I wonder if the regime change in Iran could have something to do with it. What freaks me out is the destruction of the Capitol Building. Some pundits think there's a link between the bombing and time travel, but I can't figure out how."

"Well, it's a beautiful day, Tim. Let's enjoy the great weather. Last I checked we're still in 2021 and I intend to stay in this year."

"So, are you looking forward to skippering your new charter yacht? Big change from serving over 2,000 passengers to entertaining six high paying guests."

"I'm totally looking forward to the change. I get paid a nice buck to drive this ship, but you can keep the stress. Just this morning I got a report from the leader of one of our large tour groups bitching about the breakfast menu. I'll be happy to leave that kind of shit behind me. Soon you'll have your own command, Tim, and you can worry about that stuff."

"Well, I'm just happy that our new government was sworn in last week. We no longer have a government consisting of only one person, although Ashley Patterson is more than qualified to be President."

"That she is, Tim, not to mention that she's also one gorgeous, sexy fox. Jack Thurber is one lucky guy."

"Hey, Skipper, what's that rumbling all about? Holy shit, where did the sunlight go? It's pitch dark. Oh my God, you don't think…"

"We've both read and heard all about what we're going through, Tim. I think we're passing through a fucking wormhole. In a couple of minutes, we'll know for sure."

Two minutes passed. The rumbling stopped and the daylight returned. But it was completely overcast, and the air felt suddenly cold.

"I recall you just saying that we should enjoy the beautiful weather, Skipper. Looks like the unthinkable has happened to the *Majesty of the Seas*. We've just travelled through time."

Chapter 47

Buster, what the hell is going on? I thought our time travel problems were done with after the regime change in Iran. But now ships are disappearing left and right. Have you been in touch with any of your pals in Tehran?"

"Yes, Madam President, I've been in touch with them, and I've spent hours on the phone just today with Prime Minister Ahmadi. They're going nuts just like we are. Just this morning, an Iranian cruise ship went missing. You heard me—an Iranian ship. From the facts, it seems definite that the ship crossed a wormhole. But who is responsible for the wormhole? It's not Iran, so who is it? Once again, we have a wormhole crisis on our hands. And so does Iran. We've got to find the bastards who are doing this. Iran is on our side 100 percent, but as of now, both Iran and the Unites States are in the dark. This shit is at the top of the CIA's crisis list. All I can say as of now, Madam President, is that we're working on it."

"Buster, work harder. We've got to stop this."

If there's one thing in the world that sucks beyond all else, it's thinking you've solved a crisis, only to find it's still staring you in the face.

Chapter 48

Good morning, ladies and gentlemen, Gayle King reporting for *CBS News*. I'm about to report a series of events that can only be described as shocking. This morning, no fewer than six giant cruise ships have disappeared. Yes, disappeared. In the past few weeks, we have heard stories about ships that suddenly went missing. All but one, the *Queen Mary 2*, have been U.S. Navy ships.

"All of the ships that went missing this morning are commercial cruise ships. What is beyond shocking is the reason the ships disappeared—time travel. Government scientists have told us that all of the ships encountered a thing called a wormhole, an invisible portal in time itself. It's hard to imagine that just a few months ago, few people ever heard of time travel. Now, it seems to be a regular part of news reports. All of the ships, except for the six that went missing this morning, have returned safely to the present.

"I have with me in the studio my *CBS* colleague, the veteran news anchor, Norah O'Donnell. Norah, as I'm sure you recall, was at the news desk when the late President, Matthew Blake, addressed the nation at the annual State of the Union Address. In an instant, as Norah reported, our government was murdered before the audience on national TV.

"Good morning, Norah. Please give us your take on this morning's horrific disappearance of six cruise ships, and how these incidents may have a connection to the State of the Union massacre."

Norah took a deep breath as she recalled her nationally televised freak-out during the State of the Union Address.

"Good morning, Gayle and thank you for inviting me on your show. I'm still getting over the worst event of my life, the State of the Union address, which you aptly called a massacre. Your humble anchorwoman turned into a babbling bonehead on national TV. The vast majority of our government was murdered in an instant by a nuclear weapon. It happened as our nation was still reeling from the stories of ship disappearances.

"Scientists tell us that the ship incidents were the result of wormholes in the ocean. A wormhole, known to science as an Einstein-Rosen Bridge, is an opening in time itself. Think of it as a portal from one age to another. Yes, time travel is no longer just a sub-genre of science fiction, but a real phenomenon. It's rare, but it happens. And we've recently discovered that a wormhole is not only a phenomenon of nature, but can be created on the earth by a signal from a satellite in space. Yes, as strange as it sounds, a wormhole can be man-made."

"Norah, please tell us how man-made time travel is related to the State of the Union tragedy, which apparently had nothing to do with time travel."

"Yes, Gayle, the State of the Union Address had nothing to do with time travel, but it had everything to do with a signal from a satellite in space. I should emphasize that all this is speculation, but it's speculation based on advanced-thinking scientists. Just as a wormhole can be created by an electronic signal, so too can a satellite send a detonation signal to a bomb on earth. No longer is there needed a missile, an airplane, or even a timing device. This brings the use of nuclear weapons to a frightening new level. Just press a button."

"Norah, please give us your thoughts on the suddenly new political situation in the country."

"Like you, Gayle, I'm a newsperson and I'm not supposed to give my political opinions. But I cannot avoid giving my opinion on this matter. Our country has been going through some traumatic times, but in one way we're fortunate. Yes, we're fortunate to have as President of the United States a leader that we could only pray for. Ashley Patterson, as we know, was not elected but came to the job as a *Designated Successor* by statute. Her name simply came up as the next in line from a list. But although she's unelected, she is a serious and dedicated head of state. She was once the nation's highest-ranking military officer, and now she's the highest-ranking political leader in the free world. God bless you, President Patterson. We need you."

Chapter 49

B ret Baier for *Fox News,* ladies and gentlemen. I often
long for the day when I can report news that isn't earth-
shattering. I miss the day when I could report a transit
strike in Chicago, a fire in an office building in New York, or
a close mayoral election in Los Angeles. But that day is long
gone, as you will see from the news I'm about to report. First
is a series of events on the world's oceans. Six cruise ships
have suddenly gone missing. Because there were no distress
messages, authorities suspect that these incidents may be yet
another story of unintended time travel. We have heard nothing
from the missing ships. They simply disappeared. We will bring
you more news about these events as the stories unfold.

"The major story tonight concerns our government. I
reported last week about the huge election to replace the
officials who were killed in the State of the Union tragedy. As
I reported, the Freedom Party, of which President Patterson
is a member, controls the Executive Branch and holds a five-
seat majority in the Senate. The most immediate impact of the
Senate results means that President Patterson's selection of
Supreme Court seats went essentially unopposed. The America
First Party has a six-member majority in the House. So, as the
Founding Fathers would have hoped, the three branches of
government are not controlled by one party. We have political

diversity and balance, although the numbers are tight.

"But today's big news about the federal government concerns its location. For over 200 years the federal government was synonymous with Washington, D.C. As of today, that is no longer the case. All three branches of government are now located at the Greenbrier Resort in White Sulphur Springs, West Virginia. Until 1993, the Greenbrier was the alternate site of government in case of a national disaster. The scheme was known by the code words 'Project Greek Island.' The plan was dissolved after a newspaper article disclosed it, destroying its secrecy.

"Well, a disaster has occurred, as we all know, with the bombing of the Capitol Building on the night of the State of the Union Address, wiping out most of the government, including the entire legislative branch, both the Senate and the House. The Greenbrier once again came into the view of the heads of government.

"The move was a massive undertaking, led by Jack Thurber, President Patterson's husband and Chief of Staff, and the new Vice President, former Army General Wayne Summers. An area in the main building, the Bunker, is where Congress will meet. The Bunker is the same location as it was during the since-defunct Project Greek Island. The physical layout of the site hasn't changed much over the years, making the project somewhat manageable. Because the Greenbrier is a resort, not a construction company, much of the physical labor was provided by government workers from the U.S. Army Corps of Engineers. The move was not a charitable effort, and the Greenbrier is compensated appropriately.

"The Greenbrier is the central location of an organization known as the *Keepers of Time*, a group dedicated to preserving the worthy aspects of Western civilization. The management of the *Keepers of Time* and the Greenbrier is a story in itself, one heavily concerned with the increasingly important subject of time travel. Bill Wellfleet is the four times great grandson of Ezekiel Wellfleet, the man who founded the *Keepers.* They look like twins, not widely intergenerational relatives. Bill Wellfleet is over 200 years old but looks not a day over 40. As I said, the Wellfleets are a story unto themselves, as is the bizarre phenomenon of time travel.

"I asked the President for her thoughts on the massive move, and, typical of President Patterson, she was forthcoming with her thinking. Welcome to my show, Madam President."

"Good evening, Bret. A pleasure to see you again. Jack and I came up with the idea of moving to West Virginia almost simultaneously. Because a brand-new government was about to be elected, we knew there would be no problem for people adjusting to a new space. The decision was largely motivated by security concerns after the tragic bombing of the Capitol Building. The physical layout of the Greenbrier readily lends itself to safety. The Greenbrier will be protected by a battalion, yes a battalion not a company, of U.S. Army regulars. That's about 1,000 soldiers. We want to avoid at all costs a repeat of the State of the Union bombing. The new Congress just approved of an exception to the Posse Comitatus Act, allowing the use of military troops in a civilian setting. The site is also protected by a squadron of heavily armed attack helicopters as well as regular fighter jet flyovers. As my friend Bill Wellfleet puts it, 'If you want to commit suicide, pick a fight with *The Keepers of Time.*' The American people can feel confident that their government will be well protected."

"Madam President, you are well known as a serious military person, until recently the highest-ranking officer in any branch. If you pardon my bluntness, I've read that you have been referred to as 'one tough customer.' Would you like to comment on being elevated to the highest office in the land?"

"Along with every American, I was shocked at the State of the Union attack. I felt flattered to be named as a statutory *Designated Successor*, also known as a *Designated Survivor*. Because I was quite far down on the list, I was amazed when I learned that I would be the one to take the job. I'm still shocked. But one thing I learned from my years in the Navy, when I'm given an assignment, I execute it to the best of my ability. I intend to do just that."

"Madam President, I thank you for appearing on our show. I believe I speak for all my fellow citizens when I say that I'm happy to have a courageous leader like you taking care of our country in these worrisome times.

"Bret Baier, signing off for *Fox News*.

Chapter 50

After we completed the move to the Greenbrier, Jack and I sat in my new office—we even made it *oval*. We met with the *Wormhole Gang*, Jenny, Jack, and Mike, along with Vice President Wayne Summers, whom I appointed as a *Gang* member. I couldn't have been happier with my vice-presidential pick. Wayne is smart, organized, and funny as hell. He freaked out when I appointed him a *Wormhole Gang*ster. "Do I get to carry a club, Madam President?"

I hated the idea that we were still living in a crisis, one that seems to get bigger every day. Our latest shock was the creation of the new wormholes. All sea captains have been trained in 'wormhole management.' They all know the procedure of recrossing a portal to get back to the time you came from. That task has been made easier with the introduction of the *Wormy*, the wormhole detection device. All ships, both civilian and military, are now equipped with a *Wormy*. But where the hell are the six ships that went missing five days ago? Given our knowledge of handling a wormhole, especially with the wonderful *Wormy* detection device, those ships should have reappeared by now. But where are they? Brilliant Jenny has a habit of coming up with answers to problems, and she came up with a theory. But I hated her theory, as compelling as it was, because it was scary as hell.

"I'm afraid we're looking at a new type of wormhole, Madam President," Jenny said. "I think the jihadis, or whoever the hell they are, have come up with a wormhole that disappears when you cross it. It gets me sick to think about it, but I'm afraid that the *Wormies* may be worthless. If a wormhole vanishes after you cross it, a *Wormy* can't detect something that no longer exists."

The room became silent. Jenny's idea, if true, is the worst scenario to contemplate. You can't recross something that isn't there.

"We need to contact the Pentagon," Jack said. "They need to turn loose their scientific brains on this new problem. I mean, shit, we may be looking at a crisis for which there's no solution."

"Jack is right, Madam President," VP Wayne said. "We need a lot of brainpower on this problem."

"But I could be wrong," Jenny said. "My idea is just a theory at this point. Maybe there is another explanation for why those ships haven't come back."

"Jen, honey," I said, "I would love for you to be wrong, but when was the last time you missed the mark? The answer is never. For the time being we're stuck. Your idea is the most logical answer. Wormholes appearing is frightening, but wormholes *disappearing* is a whole new ballgame."

So, here we are in our beautiful new surroundings at the Greenbrier, facing a crisis worse than the one we thought we defeated. Disappearing wormholes? Can things get any worse?

At least we now have a full government.

Chapter 51

Captain Cyrus Drake stood on the bridge of his ship, *The Sea Dragon* with his First Officer, James Pearsall. *The Sea Dragon* is a 75,000-ton, 900-foot cruise ship with a passenger count of 2,500 people. Ten hours ago, she tossed off her lines in Miami and steamed for the Caribbean. Suddenly, Captain Drake regretted they had gotten underway.

"This shit is impossible, Jim. A few short weeks ago we thought we had the wormhole problem licked with that amazing detection device, the *Wormy*. But the problem seems to have gotten worse, at least for us. We've tried to recross what we thought was the friggin wormhole a dozen times, but here we are in God knows what year. Those prehistoric sharks we've spotted tells me we're far from the time we came from. The bottom line is that we've crossed a wormhole that doesn't enable detection, and therefore doesn't allow recrossing. I hope you like dinosaurs."

"Captain, I'm stumped. In the past few months, the world became painfully aware of time travel, and that includes our passengers. They know the score and they're scared shitless. So am I. I had lunch in the passenger dining room, and I couldn't believe my ears. A lot of those people are blaming *you* for causing something over which you had no control. Royal

Caribbean never taught us how to handle a mutiny, and I'm afraid that's what we're facing. Unless we can figure out what to do, we have a huge problem on our hands. My job is to assist you and give you my thinking, but I'm afraid that I've run out of ideas. As I've been trained, I took a fix as soon as I felt that rumbling and it got dark. I'm sure we crossed the very same spot, a dozen times as you said, but here we are, lost in time."

"Looks like we're in serious trouble. Ever since time travel began hitting the newspapers, we thought we had a handle on the problem. But this one's a bitch. I've never heard of a wormhole you can't recross. But now we can't even find the goddam thing, even with our wormhole detecting device. I think we're fucked—big time."

Chapter 52

Madam President, I'm afraid we have a problem, a big one," Jenny said. Jack and I were sitting in the (new) Oval Office when Jenny almost ran into the room. "Another cruise ship has gone missing and the other six ships that disappeared are still gone. It's been 10 days since the first ship vanished. Over 28,000 passengers and crew are somewhere out there, God knows where or in what time."

I looked at Jack and could tell we were both thinking the same thing. Sometimes I hate meetings, but we obviously needed one.

"Jenny, call Admiral Wayman, the Chief of Naval Operations, and ask him to come here now. Also, please ask Vice President Summers to come. I know he's in a meeting, but he needs to be here."

"How about Rear Admiral Mike Dunton, the Defense Department science boss?" Jack said. "He's the wormhole detection maven, or we thought he was."

"Yes, we need to talk to him, Jack. Those wonderful *Wormies* of his don't appear to be working. A couple of weeks ago we had begun to look at a wormhole as a minor inconvenience, but now it's once again a crisis. I think that 28,000 people lost in time is definitely a crisis."

Jack walked into an alcove to make his phone calls. On his way, he leaned over, squeezed my hand, and kissed me. My heart does a leap when he does that. "I love you, honey," he said.

"Don't you mean Madam President?" I said, pinching his butt.

"I love you, Madam Wiseass."

"Much better."

———————

Chief of Naval Operations Wayman was on a flight to San Diego and couldn't make our meeting. VP Wayne Summers walked in followed by the DOD scientist Mike Dunton. Jack had briefed them on our problem before they arrived. Jack had contacted Buster from the CIA to be there as well. Jenny and Mike, the *Wormhole Gang*, were there too. What better meeting for a *Wormhole Gang*ster than one that discusses a broken down *Wormy*.

"It looks like your wormhole detectors are pieces of shit," VP Wayne said to Admiral Dunton. General Wayne loves to get to the point.

"Touché, Mr. Vice President," Dunton said, "but in our defense, the DOD is as shocked as anyone else. We're now worse off than we were before."

"How are we worse off?" I asked. I wanted specifics not generalities.

"Well, Madam President, before we invented the *Wormy*, as you and Captain Jack call it, we didn't know we were on a wormhole before we encountered it. Now, we don't know where a wormhole is even after we cross the goddam thing. We thought we had a simple solution—just recross the portal and you're back to where you came from. Simple, yes? But no. Now when you cross a wormhole you're lost in time, and the worst part is you don't know how to return to the present. Those seven lost cruise ships bear that out. The first group of six have been missing for a week, and the most recent one for 24 hours. This is a crisis worse than we could have imagined. It seems that VP Summers was correct that the device is a piece of shit."

"Mike, please pardon General Wayne for jumping on your butt. Once a soldier, always a soldier, I guess."

I've taken to heart Jack's constant admonitions that I should "make nice." Here I was making nice for somebody else. That's okay, I want everyone on my team to know that his ass isn't always on the line. Often, but not always.

"No need for an apology, Madam President," Mike Dunton said, "I'm afraid that General Wayne just may be correct that our wormhole detection device, or *Wormy* as you call it, is a piece of shit. At least it behaved that way in the past week. As I said before, we're now in worse shape than we were in at the beginning of the crisis. A disappearing wormhole is worse than one you can't detect."

"I'm sorry to bust your balls, Admiral Dunton," VP Wayne said, "but we're all a bit on edge over this problem. Any thoughts on what we can do to unscramble the eggs?"

"As of right now, all we can do is go over our findings, rework the engineering, and try to come up with an answer."

Jenny raised her hand, which didn't surprise me.

"What about omnidirectional sonar? It's one of the best

pieces of technology on any ship. You can detect not only what's under you, but anything within 360 degrees. If we can somehow figure out how to hook up shipboard sonar with the wormhole detector, we may be on our way to solving the problem."

The room went silent. Oh, my God, could it be that Jenny has come up with a solution to a problem that seems unsolvable? She's done it before, so why not now?

I stood and walked over to Jenny's seat and poured her a cup of coffee. I wanted everyone to be clear how high a regard I have for Jenny, and the Commander in Chief pouring her coffee did just that.

"Jenny, no surprise, has whacked us upside our heads with a solution out of left field. Jen, honey, please explain your thoughts."

"Well, as I recall when Admiral Dunton first told us about DOD's work on a wormhole detecting device, it was based in large part on omnidirectional sonar technology. Maybe we should go back to the beginning of the experiments and work sonar into our thinking. Something tells me it may do the trick. Also, Buster can turn loose his insiders to see if we're on the right track."

"I'm working on it in my head already," Buster said. When Jenny has an idea, people take notice, and, more often than not, take action.

Sonar. Who would have thought that? Jenny would have thought that.

"Madam President, I hope I'm not being out of line by asking this question, but

Do we have any idea what country or group is behind this?"

Jenny said.

"At one time it was Iran, but since the regime change, we're now on the same side, but neither Iran nor us can figure out who the enemy is. But there's a big problem. As of right now 28,000 people are lost in time on cruise ships. What if whoever is behind this has the capability of attacking them? I don't want to risk their lives. Therefore, I want to see if Jenny's brilliant sonar idea works before I consider military action of any sort, especially because we don't know who the target is."

Chapter 53

Jack keeps reminding me that I'm the Commander in Chief, and I shouldn't get myself involved in day-to-day operations. But I can't help it. I'm a techie at heart and I have a deep-seated need to know what's going on from the inside. The Navy tells its officers that their most important task is "attention to detail." I always followed that advice as a naval officer, and I've taken it with me to the Oval Office. God knows I'm surrounded by big-brained people, especially Jack and Jenny, but I always want to grab for the controls. That's the way I am, and I'm not about to change. So, my *Gang* will just need to put up with my hands-on involvement. I try not to be a pain in the ass, but try as I may, it's who I am—a pain in the ass.

Jenny, our resident genius, may have just come up with the answer to our friggin wormhole problem, specifically man-made wormholes. My God, her idea that omnidirectional sonar may be a key is typical of Jenny, typical meaning brilliant. My years on the bridge of warships have made me quite familiar with sonar technology, and I think Jenny may really be on to something—really.

So, with my fondness for giving names to groups, I named the committee that worked on Jenny's sonar idea, the Sonar Committee. Imaginative, no? Large groups working on a mission can often get bogged down in cross firing and confusion, so I kept the committee small. It consists of Jack as chairman, Rear Admiral Mike Dunton of the DOD Science Department, VP Wayne Summers, and me. I also included Buster of the CIA in our plans. Jenny and Mike, the *Wormhole Gangsters,* are on the committee, of course, especially because it was Jenny's idea. Jack is accustomed to working with me after our many Navy missions together.

I promised him that I wouldn't be a pain in the ass, which he appreciated but didn't believe a word of it. Mike Dunton, the DOD scientist, is the technical honcho of the group. Mike has a bunch of sharp people working for him, and, along with them and the committee, he focused on the sonar/wormhole issue like a laser. I personally like these folks, and I love Jack, so working with them will be a pleasure. A pleasure? Yes, keeping our country from being destroyed is a pleasure, if a somewhat scary one.

Chapter 54

I think I've done a good job about keeping my promise to Jack not to be a pain in the ass. But, truth be told, my years as a senior naval officer have given me a pretty good handle on technical nautical matters, including, most specifically, omnidirectional sonar. Rear Admiral Mile Dunton, the DOD scientist, appreciated my input. So did Jack. Whenever I made some good points at a meeting, Jack would always pinch me on the ass and kiss me when the meeting ended, after making sure nobody was watching. We may be involved in a critical national security problem, but Jack and I are, well, Jack and me. Have I mentioned how much I love Jack, *my* Jack?

Following on the heels of my predecessor, President Matt Blake, I declared a National State of Emergency. Going to sea and disappearing into another time sure as hell qualifies as an emergency. As Commander in Chief, no fucking way will I put up with this shit. My commitment to curb my salty language is not going well.

Jack walked into the Oval Office, having just come from a Sonar Committee meeting at the Pentagon.

"So, tell me when we can book a sea cruise," my wise-ass mouth inquired.

"We're making progress, hon, serious progress. We've gone through the mathematical analysis and computer simulations and will be ready to do live testing next week."

"That will make it three weeks since those seven ships went missing, Jack, along with 28,000 passengers and crew, mainly American. Those people are ultimately my responsibility and it gets me sick that they're somewhere out there lost in time. And we don't even know what era they're in. My patience is wearing thin."

"My gut tells me we're about to round the corner, honey. You put together one hell of a committee. Your position as Chief Pain-in-the-Ass helps move this mission forward."

"So, here's a direct order, Captain. Gimme a kiss."

Chapter 55

Joint Base Andrews-Naval Air Facility Washington, better known as Joint Base Andrews and abbreviated to JBA, is a United States military facility located in Prince George's County, Maryland. The base is under the jurisdiction of the United States Air Force 316th Wing, Air Force District of Washington. The base was established in 2009, when Andrews Air Force Base and the Naval Air Facility, Washington were merged. Like most people, I still think of the place simply as Andrews Air Force Base. I know the base well because that's where Air Force One is located. I'm still having a hard time getting the idea that the beautiful 747 changes its name from Boeing VC-25 to Air Force One when I'm aboard. Actually, Air Force One isn't just one plane, but is the name for any plane when I'm aboard. Hot shit, no?

Today, the Sonar Committee is gathered there for the first live test of the satellite that we hope will solve the *Wormhole Crisis*. To say that a lot is weighing on this project is an understatement. A new rocket launch facility was built at Andrews for security reasons. Cape Canaveral, the normal site for a rocket launch, is just too publicly known, and this operation requires strict secrecy. Our objective is simple—to control wormhole creation. Getting to that objective is anything but simple, but I'm confident that Admiral Dunton and his team of propeller heads in the DOD Science Department know what they're doing. Besides brains, Mike Dunton is known for his dedication to getting a job done.

The launch vehicle is a modified SS-520 rocket, a dependable piece of technology with a proven track record. We inserted our ear plugs as the launch officer announced that he was about to light off the engine. The ground rumbled as the rocket took off. My experience with wormholes always makes my stomach rumble along with the sound of a rocket launch.

We all instinctively applauded when the first stage of the rocket detached and fell away. Jenny, the brain behind the sonar theory, broke into a spontaneous Lindy with Mike, which was quite a challenge without music.

The satellite, which Jenny christened as *Wormblaster,* successfully took its position in space.

Admiral Mike had two objectives for today's test. First is to detect a wormhole. Secondly, and this was an ambitious goal, to *create* a wormhole. If we can do that, we have ourselves a time machine. But our overarching objective is to find the seven missing cruise ships. If we can't accomplish that, 28,000 people, most of them Americans, will never be heard from again. No way will I let that happen.

Forty-five minutes after the successful launch of *Wormblaster,* we achieved objective number one—We found a wormhole. Now we would execute our rescue plan, or at least try. I had ordered Admiral Jake Wayman, the Chief of Naval Operations, to assign seven frigates for the mission of leading the missing cruise ships back through the wormholes. A frigate, which was my first at-sea command, is best understood as a large destroyer. Since we first encountered the wormhole problem, I had ordered, in my position as Fleet Admiral at the time, that a numerical designation be attached to any wormhole we discovered. So, we have locations, identities, and the knowledge of where the wormhole leads in time. This is the key to rescuing any ship that encountered a wormhole. Admiral Jake is a sharp guy, and readily grasped what I was up to. We recognized the obvious, that the mission for the assigned frigates was not without serious risk, so Jake issued a request for volunteers. We were surprised, but not shocked, when we had an overwhelming positive response for volunteers. People are fascinated by time travel, and that includes brave U.S. Navy sailors. We have more volunteers than we need.

We identified the wormhole as WH106 off the coast of southern New Jersey. Admiral Jake assigned the *USS Taylor* as the rescue ship, an Oliver Hazard Perry class frigate. Its mission was to cross wormhole WH106 and try to contact the *Majesty of the Seas,* the Royal Caribbean cruise ship we believe crossed that wormhole.

As we monitored the operation over our radio, the *Taylor* steamed up and down the coast, all the while trying to hail the *Majesty.* Captain Dwight Maxwell repeated his constant message. "This is the *USS Taylor* calling the *Majesty of the Seas.* Come in, please."

He finally got a reply.

"This is the *Majesty,* Captain James Gordon speaking, read you loud and clear," came the breathless message.

"Follow me, Captain Jim. We're about to visit the year 2021."

Oh my God, it looks like we did it.

The *Taylor* led the *Majesty* and her 2,500 passengers through the wormhole and steamed for Clinton Wharf in Brooklyn. The wharf had seven assigned piers for the wormhole rescue project.

With this one ship, the *Majesty of the Seas*, we discovered how to rescue all the other ships.

The Sonar Committee screamed and cheered like a bunch of school kids. From my years in the Navy, I've never forgotten the feeling when you accomplish a mission, and we sure as hell accomplished this one. I told (asked) Jack to put in all of the committee members for Presidential Citations, and to award Jenny, the brain behind the operation, the Presidential Medal of Freedom. I wouldn't make the announcement just yet. I invited the committee to the Greenbrier/White House for a good old-fashioned party to celebrate one of the most amazing accomplishments to date. I handed out the awards in the new Oval Office. When I pinned Jenny with the Presidential Medal of Freedom, I read the words on the award:

"The Presidential Medal of Freedom is awarded an especially meritorious contribution to the security or national interests of the United States, world peace, cultural or other significant public or private endeavors."

"You have more than earned this award, Jenny," I said.

Mike wrapped his arms around her as Jenny quietly wept.

The *Wormhole Crisis* is no longer a crisis.

Chapter 56

Our second wedding anniversary is next week. Jack, sweetheart that he is, always figures out a way to buy me a special gift for any occasion. We were still reeling from our successful defeat of the *Wormhole Crisis, and* something told me this gift would be extra special. As talented as he is with managing money, Jack casts that aside when buying me a gift. Have I mentioned how much I love Jack?

"Hey, Madam President, I mean baby, why don't we round up some Secret Service guys and take a helicopter to Washington, where we'll have a nice picnic lunch on the Potomac?"

Jack, the relentless romantic, came up with a typically great idea.

"That's a wonderful plan. Lead the way, honey."

We climbed into Marine One, my helicopter. When we landed in the parking area on the Potomac, I noticed a huge red, white, and blue tarpaulin stretched along one of the piers. Two Secret Service Agents stood at each side of the tarp. My heart told me that something special was behind that tarpaulin.

Jack put his arm around me, pulled me close, and said, "Happy anniversary, honey. You're the best."

He nodded to one of the Secret Service guys who pulled on a rope. The tarp fell to the dock.

"Oh, my God, Jack, you're too much. Is this my anniversary gift?"

"It sure is, and no President deserves it more than you."

Tied up to the dock was the beautiful old Presidential Yacht, *The Sequoia.*

"Penny-pinching Jimmy Carter sold it, and I just bought it back. It's all yours, baby. Let's climb aboard, Madam Sweetheart."

As we climbed the short gangplank, none other than Mike and Jenny stood there. Mike held a microphone and announced, "United States of America, arriving."

"Welcome to *The USS Sequoia,* Madam President," Jenny said.

"How about some history, Jenny," Jack said. Jenny, no surprise, had taught herself everything there is to know about the presidential yacht.

Jenny first read from a Congressional Resolution passed in December 1985.

"Sequoia was the setting for Presidential meetings, negotiations, and decisions of extraordinary significance for and effect on the history of the United States and the course of world events and is recognized for its unique significance. The former Presidential yacht *Sequoia* has made itself a symbol of American political heritage and the Office of the President."

Jack outdid himself with this gift. He sure as hell knows how to spend money. Fortunately, he has a ton of it.

Jenny continued, telling us the history of the *Sequoia* as

only she can.

"The *Sequoia* was launched in 1925. At 104 feet in length with a beam of 18 feet, *Sequoia's* hull was originally constructed of yellow pine on white oak frames, and her deckhouse is built of mahogany and teak. She draws 4.5 feet under her and weighs 90 tons. Her cruising speed is 12 knots. She is capable of comfortably sleeping eight guests in her three double and two single staterooms and can seat 22 for formal dinners. During Prohibition, *Sequoia* was used to patrol the Chesapeake and Delaware Bays as a decoy vessel to attract would-be bootleggers. Something tells me that your anniversary gift won't be booze-free, Madam President.

"The *Sequoia* first saw presidential duty during the Hoover administration, which also coincided with Prohibition. In a goofy display of ignoring Prohibition, Hoover included a picture of his yacht on Christmas cards he sent out in 1932. I doubt that people struggling to make rent appreciated the President's yacht.

"President Franklin Roosevelt made good use of the *Sequoia*. Besides fishing, he used it for a site of important meetings and summits.

"As the world political situation became uncertain with Hitler and the Japanese militarists, the wooden *Sequoia* was deemed unsafe for the President, and on December 9, 1935, *Sequoia* was officially reassigned to the Secretary of the Navy and the steel-hulled *USS Potomac* was designated as the presidential yacht. For the next few years, *Sequoia* served at the pleasure of the United States Secretary of Navy until its recommissioning as a presidential yacht.

"On election to the Presidency, Eisenhower ordered his Joint Chiefs of Staff to meet on the *Sequoia* to develop a plan for implementing Eisenhower›s 'New Look' defense policy. A document known as The *Sequoia* Report helped introduce a defense strategy to reduce the overall size and cost of the military and rely heavily on nuclear deterrence, a doctrine that would serve as a defining turning point in U.S. strategy during the Cold War. No doubt about it, Madam President, this boat has seen its share of history.

"During the Kennedy administration, the *Sequoia* was the site of strategy meetings to discuss the Cuban Missile Crisis. Kennedy was scheduled to host friends for a dinner cruise on November 24, 1962. He was assassinated two days before that planned voyage.

"President Lyndon Johnson loved the *Sequoia*. Records showed that he took 34 recorded cruises. Typical of hard-living Johnson, he had a wet bar installed to replace the elevator that polio-stricken Franklin Roosevelt had ordered.

"No President used the *Sequoia* more than Richard Nixon, who took no fewer than 84 voyages. In a 1983 interview titled, 'The Smoking Gun and the *Sequoia*' Nixon describes a cruise aboard the *Sequoia* during which he learned that a court had ordered him to release the transcript of a tape recording that showed he approved the cover-up of the Watergate break-in. Wow, the *Sequoia* even played a role in Watergate.

"President Gerald Ford was the first known president to host a Cabinet meeting aboard the vessel. Ford celebrated his 62nd birthday on the *Sequoia*.

"President Jimmy Carter sold the *Sequoia* at auction after the ship had seen 46 years of government service. Records showed that the *Sequoia* cost the taxpayers $800,000 per year. He would later regret his decision, when he realized that the American people loved the Sequoia.

"Madam President, with Jack manning the checkbook, I don't think you'll need to be a penny pincher like the Peanut Farmer from Georgia.

"*Sequoia* was most recently owned by FE Partners, a company in Washington D.C., which purchased *Sequoia* in October 2016 for $7.8 million. Jack bought *Sequoia* for $8 million."

Jenny looked at Jack. "Please don't be pissed off at me for disclosing that, Jack. I read it in the *Washington Post.*"

"So that, Madam President, is what the *Sequoia* is all about. Your wonderful husband just bought you a piece of American history as your anniversary present."

I broke down in tears. How could I not? Jack has a way of making life special, and Jenny has a way of telling the story. Jack encouraged Jenny to put all her research into a book, which Thurber Publishing will happily bring to life. Jenny loves the idea.

I called VP Wayne Summers and his wife Gayle. I wanted to include them on the first cruise of my anniversary present. Since I picked Wayne as my second in command, Jack and I have taken a liking for those two. With Mike at the helm, we took the *Sequoia* on a short maiden cruise under her new owner—me.

What can be more fun than a cruise on a beautiful yacht?

We shall see.

Chapter 57

We motored down the Potomac and headed for Chesapeake Bay. Jack held my hand and took me on a tour of the *Sequoia*. At 104 feet in length, the yacht is large, but by no means gigantic. I recently commanded the *USS Gerald R. Ford*, the largest aircraft carrier ever built, so size is a relative thing to the beholder. The vessel is beautiful, no doubt about it. But besides its physical beauty, the *Sequoia* just oozed history, a quality that I love. Just as when we moved into the White House, I felt like I was part of something big. Hoover, Roosevelt, Truman, Eisenhower, Kennedy, Johnson, Nixon, Ford, Carter. Wow, those names rang through my ears as we toured the staterooms. The master suite isn't what Moneybags Jack usually likes, but it had a wonderful historical quality to it. This is no simple boat.

"Hey."

"Hey what?"

"I love you. I can't possibly imagine a nicer anniversary gift. What have you got planned for my birthday?"

"A receipt for *Sequoia* marked 'paid in full.'"

We had just entered Chesapeake Bay and the waves picked

up a bit. But the solid old yacht took to the water perfectly. We walked up to the bridge. Being accustomed to the bridge on the gigantic *Ford*, I was once again reminded that size is relative. Much of the Chesapeake is quite shallow, with 24 percent of the bay less than six feet, and an average depth of 21 feet. Because the *Sequoia* draws only 4.5 feet, I wasn't worried, especially with Mike at the helm. He has a radar and sonar device between his ears. We were all on the bridge, Jenny and Mike, the Summers, Jack, and me. It was a beautiful day with not a cloud in the sky, although the water was a bit choppy.

Gayle Summers looked at Jack and said, "Hey, Jack, please give Wayne a seminar on how to pick out gifts. This yacht is absolutely beautiful. The President is one lucky girl."

Jenny, multi-talented Jenny, took out her guitar and sang "God Bless America."

Perfect day. Beautiful weather, great people, a successful end to a dangerous crisis, and a wonderful yacht. Although my job comes with its share of worries, I thought, what can possibly go wrong?

I felt a soft rumble under me. When I looked at the water, I noticed that the chop had disappeared, and we were in calm water. But the rumbling continued and became stronger. The beautiful cloudless sky suddenly darkened and then turned pitch black. We went from daylight to darkness.

I'm the President of the United States, and I constantly remind myself to put on the proverbial stiff upper lip for those around me. But my stiff upper lip was quivering. I glanced at Jack, who looked like I felt—scared.

"Jack, honey, you don't think..."

"No, I don't *think*, baby, I *know*. And I don't like what I know.

And *you* know the same thing."

I tried to remember my commitment to not using foul language, but I suddenly forgot.

"We just crossed a wormhole, a *fucking wormhole.*"

Characters – *The Wormhole Crisis*

Ahmadi, Farhad – Foreign Minister of Iran

Barrett, Luke – Captain of the *USS Gerald R. Ford*

Baier, Bret – News Anchorman – *Fox News*

Blake, Dee – First Lady of the United States

Blake, Jenny – Member of the Wormhole Gang

Blake, Matt – President of the United States

Blackwell, Maggie – Aide to Past President Conklin

Boyle, Tim – Head of the Secret Service

Buster – CIA Director, aka Charles Atkins

Campbell, Jeremy – First Lieutenant, *HMS Endeavor*

Chung, Mi-Ki – Chinese trade official, aka, *Micky*

Conklin, George – Former President of the United States

Drake, Cyrus – Captain, *the Sea Dragon*

Dunton, Michael –Chief of DOD Science Department

Ferguson, Miles – Navy SEAL platoon leader from the *Ford*.

Frank, Mildred – Leader, America First Party

Ghorbani, Ahura – Iranian Prime Minister

Hart, Max – CIA Agent, brother-in-law to Ahmad Rafshandi

Hart, Yasamin – Wife of Max Hart

Jackson, Mike – Charter Member of the Wormhole Gang

King, Gayle - News anchorwoman for *CBS*

Kingsmith, Nigel – Commanding Officer, *HMS Endeavor*

Marsden, Nancy – Former Senator and White House Counsel

Mohammadi, Hashem – Deputy Foreign Minister of Iran

O'Donnell, Nora – News anchorwoman for *CBS*

Parker, Elizabeth – Captain of *USS Oliver Hazard Perry*

Rafshandi, Ahmad – Iranian Deputy Prime Minister

Rafshandi, Donia – Ahmad's wife

Rooney, Alex – Justice of the Supreme Court

Summers, Gayle – Wayne's wife

Summers, Wayne – Retired General, VP of the US

Tomkins, Sam – Leader, Freedom Party

Watson, Sarah – FBI Director

Wayman, Jake – Admiral, Chief of Naval Operations

Wellfleet, Bill – Leader, *The Keepers of Time,*

Wellfleet, Ezekiel – Founder of *The Keepers of Time*

Westerbeke, Bill – Captain, *Queen Mary 2*

ACKNOWLEDGEMENTS

As always, I thank my wife, Lynda, for her attentive reading, rereading, and editing of my many drafts. Lynda is to me as Ashley is to Jack. I also thank my friend and editor, John White, for his keen editorial eye—John doesn't miss a trick and picks up major and minor things that I missed. Karen Sobel, an expert beta reader, put in her Usual stellar performance. I also thank Frank Orzo, my good friend since elementary school, for his excellent comments. I thank LuAnn T. Palazzo for her interior, cover designs, and suggested edits. And I especially thank my readers, many of whom are a constant source of inspiration and encouragement for me. I cherish their comments.

THE BOOKS OF RUSS MORAN

I hope you enjoyed reading *The Wormhole Crisis as* much as I enjoyed writing it.

This book, as well as all my books are available on Amazon.com, and also as ebooks on the Kindle or a Kindle app on your smartphone or iPad.

Here are my other books you may be interested in.

THE TIME MAGNET NOVELS
The Gray Ship – **Book One** *of the Time Magnet Novels*
http://amzn.to/16GPumH

A number one Amazon best seller.

*"This **provocative, intensely powerful** novel is a must-read for sci-fi fans and Civil War aficionados, though mainstream fiction readers will find it **heart-rending and inspiring** as well. A rare read that's not only **wildly entertaining, but also profoundly moving."** –* Kirkus Reviews

The Thanksgiving Gang – **Book Two** *of the Time Magnet Novels*
The Sequel to *The Gray Ship.* A story of time travel.
http://amzn.to/1NzBs7N

"I had never read a book before written in an efficient, minimalistic prose. Instead of writing what most readers want to read, he gives voice to life-like characters, with their flaws and prejudices. They are not infallible superheroes. It's always nice to find a new voice in fiction and to enjoy creativity at its best." – C. Ludewig

"Breakneck pacing and virtually nonstop action" – Kirkus Reviews

A Time of Fear – **Book Three** *of the Time Magnet Novels*
http://amzn.to/1zdjaG9

In a month, five American cities will be devastated by suitcase nuclear bombs.

The time travelers take on their old name, The Thanksgiving Gang. They know what will happen because they travelled to the future. They know what the result will be. They've seen the devastation. They know the details. Five American cities are targeted by nuclear suitcase bombs. BUT they don't know where the bombs are – and don't know how to find them. The clock is ticking, and millions will soon lose their lives – unless they find the bombs.

"His story is fascinating, and adds even more depth to this already cavernously deep novel. Amazingly unique, chilling and well written, Moran weaves a future that is both desperate and hopeful. Blending modern fears with science fiction results in a tale that will keep you reading long into the night. Five stars!" — Heather

The Skies of Time – **Book Four** *of the Time Magnet Novels*
http://amzn.to/1CCC3jg

In *The Skies of Time*, you will recognize the two main characters, Ashley Patterson, now an admiral, and her husband, Jack Thurber. They met and fell in love in *The Gray Ship*, and now they're in for the adventure of their lives in *The Skies of Time*. Ashley and Jack have been such prominent characters in all four books of The Time Magnet Series that I feel like they're old friends. You will also recognize some of the other characters. But if I told you who they are, it would ruin the fun.

"I'm big fan of this series and this one may be the best. I hope there is another book to this series since it keeps getting better. There are a few

questions I have about certain events that makes the next one even more suspenseful. These are great books to binge read one after the other." — Time Travel Fan

The Keepers of Time *–* **Book Five** *of the Time Magnet Novels*
http://amzn.to/2wjVSTt

Admiral Ashley Patterson and her husband Jack have done it again. They've traveled through time, 200 years into the future—aboard a nuclear aircraft carrier, the *USS Ronald Reagan*, Ashley's flagship.

They discover a new world, a strange new world—a post-nuclear war world—one that is both a beacon of hope, and a cry of despair.

They meet a group of people who call themselves *The Keepers of Time,* an organization dedicated to preserving history and culture amid the horrors of a dystopian future.

The world around them has harkened back to a primitive and savage past, one that includes human sacrifice.

Ashley knows they must have to get back to the present to warn the government of the unspeakable horrors that await. But finding the way back to the present is their greatest challenge, an almost insurmountable one.

"The Keepers of Time is a really interesting take on current geopolitical events and where they are leading. From reading previous books in the series, the cast of characters is as familiar as the people next door and it was great to reconnect with them. Moran's legal background illuminates what happens when our legal structure disappears, and he has zeroed in on an essential thing about civilization – records of the past. A great read!" – Robert Shearer

THE PATTERNS SERIES
The Shadows of Terror – Book One
http://amzn.to/1IDQzJS

"A stunning page turner. A novel that explodes off the front page of your newspaper."

Terrorism has a new face, a face that's obscured in the shadows. The radical forces of destruction have learned to make themselves invisible to the West, and preventing a terrorist attack has become almost impossible. A new war has begun, World War III.

Rick Bellamy, an FBI agent who specializes in counterterrorism, is engaged in his own war, a war with no end. Bellamy's wife, Ellen, a prominent architect, discovers that she's in the middle of the greatest terror plot to date. To defeat the enemy, Bellamy first has to uncover the clues, to shine a light on the shadows. He has to find patterns – before it's too late.

"Move over James Patterson and Mary Higgins Clark. There's a new guy in town. Russ Moran's new book – The Shadows of Terror."
— Frank O.

The Scent of Revenge - Book Two in *The Patterns Series*
http://amzn.to/2tneIsg

The world is at war with the forces of terror. FBI Agent Rick Bellamy and his wife, Ellen, find themselves in the middle of a sinister terrorist plot. Someone is attacking prominent young women, inflicting a horrible disease. Nobody knows its origin, nobody knows how to stop it, nobody knows how to cure it.

Rick Bellamy and a team of scientists want to go on the

offense. But how?

Will the lives of the women be changed forever? When will the attacks stop?

"Heart-pounding can't put down thriller that will force you to look at terrorism in different light. Life in America will never be the same." – Cold Coffee Café

A Reunion in Time – Book Three of *The Patterns Series*
http://amzn.to/2tneIsg

What if a 37-year-old adult travels back 20 years in time and finds himself in high school, followed by his 36-year-old wife? They're now teenagers, 17 and 16. Adults in teenage bodies, they struggle to convince the people from their past that they are real, not apparitions. With the benefit of hindsight, they know the history of the past 20 years, and it isn't pretty.

Rick and Ellen are married, and now must adjust to married life as teenagers in 2001. Rick is a senior FBI official and Ellen is a famous architect.

But everybody sees them as kids. Nobody believes that they're married, and nobody believes their stories—until Rick and Ellen predict 9/11.

How do they find their way back to the year they came from? How do they warn the authorities of the cataclysm that will occur in the future? The answer is to find the time portal—the wormhole—that brought them to 2001. But the site has changed. It's no longer the place where they crossed the wormhole. Will they live out the balance of their lives beginning as teenagers?

"We've all wished we could go back to earlier times with the mind

we have now. This Moran book takes you there and it is a fun creative romp well worth reading. A Reunion in Time is highly recommended!"
– Kindle customer

THE MATT BLAKE MYSTERIES
Sideswiped – **Book One in** *The Matt Blake Mysteries, a series of legal thrillers*
http://amzn.to/1MkxX35

Trial lawyer Matt Blake took on a perfect case. It involved a sideswipe collision in which his client's husband, an investigative reporter, was killed. The evidence of negligence was overwhelming. Eyewitnesses testified that defendant was talking on his cell phone when he hit the other car.

But was it negligence? Was it an accident? Or was it murder?

Matt uncovers evidence that the act may have been intentional. Somebody wanted the man silenced. Somebody wanted the man dead. Somebody had a lot to hide. The signs started to point to the highest levels of government. An open-and-shut personal injury case suddenly became a vast conspiracy of terror.

"This book hooks you in from the first line. Sideswiped draws you into the world of Matt Blake and you become emotionally attached to him and his journey. The story itself is so well-written and moves quickly. There is never a dull moment." – Sarah Elle

"Moran demonstrates the depth of his writing talent by developing a new genre with Sideswiped, a legal thriller. Branching out from his previous novels dealing with time travel, Moran goes in a whole new direction with Book One in the Matt Blake series. He creates a wild but totally believable story of modern-day intrigue and suspense. Moran also deftly weaves into this book some of my favorite characters

from his prior novels. I am looking forward to starting Book #2 - The Reformers." – Frank from Lynbrook

The Reformers – Book Two of *The Matt Blake Mysteries*
http://amzn.to/2m8uMdu

The forces of radical Islam are on the run. Their leadership has been decimated, their ranks thinned, their power disappearing by the week. Their recruiting efforts have been cut off, the radical websites shut down, and the attraction of jihad is losing its appeal among the young. With targeted assassinations, military strikes, as well as the loss of oil fields and gold mines, radical Islam is fast losing power.

But who is responsible? It isn't the United States Government. It's a new force the world has never seen before.

Lawyer Matt Blake and his wife Diana find themselves in the middle of the most gigantic plot the world has ever seen, a conspiracy that's only begun to grow.

"I've been a fan of the author, Russell Moran, since reading Sideswiped a few months ago, so I admittedly went into this book with quite high expectations. That being said, I had no idea that "The Reformers" was going to play out in the way that it does and I can see myself giving this book a re-read in the future. In fact, I am even more impressed by the storyline of this read than the last and it has left me excited to see more." – Lucidity.

"Time flies when you're scared out of your mind. The author's superb writing skills will quickly draw you into the story. Forty-two fast paced chapters will keep turning the pages of this novel until the end. Well-developed cast of realistic characters that you will relate to one will keep you engaged. One of my favorite things about Moran's books is his entire cast of characters detailed in the back of the book. I admit to

reading about the cast first in order to firmly get everyone in my mind. As a follower of his, I know each character is important to the plot and I don't want to miss anything or overlook anyone." – Cold Coffee Cafe

The President is Missing – **Book Three of** *The Matt Blake Mysteries*
http://amzn.to/2t9v7wu

While he was addressing the nation from a submerged nuclear submarine, President Blake's message is suddenly cut off. Anyone listening heard an explosion. The explosion was followed by floating debris five minutes later.

First Lady Dee Blake has doubts, which she shares with naval high command and the new president. She thinks the explosion and the debris were a ruse to make people think the sub was destroyed, and her husband with it.

Could the sub have been hijacked and the president kidnapped? But who would commit such an act? What is its purpose? Was it Russia, China, Iran, or a shadowy group of freelance terrorists?

The new president appoints Dee as his Chief of Staff, with explicit instructions to find the missing submarine—and President Matt Blake.

Her life, and the life of the nation, suddenly take a horrifying turn.

"Russ Moran wrote a true thriller, with a strong plot and even stronger characters. To think that there are good guys—Russian Naval Admirals, no less—made this book not only a solid who-done-it but also a strong 'why did they do it?'" – Unka Heshie

A Climate of Doubt – **Book Four of** *The Matt Blake Mysteries*
https://amzn.to/2OSwcHR

Forget what you ever heard about climate change. Forget your preconceived notions about reality itself. Instantly, you are in a new world, a horrifying world, a world you don't understand.

On a hot summer day, Homeland Security Secretary, Rick Bellamy, and his wife Ellen, a famous TV talk show host, walked along the ocean front trying to escape the heat. Suddenly the temperature dropped from the high 90s to below freezing in a matter of minutes. It began to snow—*on July 16*. The temperatures across the country and the world plummeted, creating winter in summer.

Bellamy and the rest of the government struggled to cope with the suddenly new climate, but to cope, they first had to find out what happened.

Scientists from academia blamed the weather on a sudden acceleration of climate change, but they were unable to explain a 60-degree temperature drop in a matter of minutes. Two astronauts in an American space station realized that the sudden weather calamity coincided with a test of the 20 satellites that the space station controlled. Attention focused on a huge American corporation that owned the space station and the satellites. Could there be a connection between the satellite tests and the radical drop in temperature?

As the deaths piled up and the world economy tilted toward disaster because of gigantic summer blizzards, Rick Bellamy and his team struggled to find answers before it was too late. Was it a sudden shift in climate change or did it have something to do with the satellites? The biggest question remained—was the catastrophe an accident, or was somebody controlling the weather? Was it terror?

"Mr. Moran does a masterful job of crafting an action-packed, suspenseful read about the devastating consequences of climate manipulation. The diabolical mastermind behind the caper is a dictator of the worst kind—a man without conscience who cares only for power. Through the magic of Mr. Moran's digital pen, the men and woman in white hats are three-dimensional and vividly real. While this is a work of fiction, it's plausible fiction. We can easily relate to the horrific consequences of such an act of terrorism as so capably portrayed in Mr. Moran's prose." – Colorado Avid Reader

THE HARRY AND MEG SERIES
The Maltese Incident – A Story of Time Travel – **Book One of** *The Harry and Meg Series,* **the prequel to** *The Violent Sea*
https://amzn.to/2RclZCT

You're on a beautiful cruise ship. The April sky is full of stars.

Suddenly, the ship rumbles, and instantly the stars disappear.

"What the hell was that?" Captain Fenton yelled. "Beats me, captain. I've never seen anything like it," the first officer said. They would soon discover that the ship, *The Maltese*, had just traveled through time—millions of years to the past.

Captain Harry Fenton, a highly decorated naval war hero, realizes the greatest battle of his life lay ahead of him. Captain Harry, a widow, falls in love with a beautiful passenger, Meg Johnson, an executive with the company that owns the ship.

After a whirlwind romance, they marry—in the ship's ballroom—100 million years in the past. Captain Harry convinces the passengers and crew that they must move ashore to a tropical island because the ship is running out of fuel and supplies. He organizes a group to go ashore and inspect the island.

An ancient forest inhabited by dinosaurs awaits them.

Meg wants to go with them. Harry, fearing for her safety, tries to convince her to stay on the ship. Meg demonstrates that she is proficient with a gun by taking apart a rifle and reassembling it—in 15 seconds. Harry marvels that he's never seen such an expert gun handler—or accurate shooter. So, AR-15 in hand, Meg joins the inspection party. Charging dinosaurs are no match for Meg Fenton's firepower.

Will the 1,000 souls ever make it back to the time they came from, or will they remain stranded in the distant past?

A scientist aboard theorizes that, to return to their present time, they need to go back to the time portal, or wormhole, that brought them to the past. But the ship doesn't have enough fuel for the journey. Realizing that their lives have hit the reset button, the crew and passengers construct a community in the forest—Malta Town.

Under Harry and Meg's leadership, they create a court system, a legislature, and all the elements of a small budding democracy. Meg figures out a way to harness hydroelectric power from a nearby waterfall. Everybody thinks of Harry and Meg as the heart and soul of Malta Town. They begin their new lives—among the dinosaurs.

The Maltese Incident is a riveting tale of time travel, love, courage, and horror.

"*As with Moran's work, he continues to be a great storyteller. I recommend reading this from title to end. It's well written, and filled with intensity and levity.*" – Amy's Bookshelf

The Violent Sea – A Story of Time Travel –* Book Two of *The Harry and Meg Series, the sequel to ***The Maltese Incident***
https://amzn.to/2AT5ypI

The Violent Sea is a novel of war, time travel, military history. It's the second book in the Harry and Meg Series. It's also a sweet romance between Harry and his wife, Meg.

Rear Admiral Harry Fenton has done it again. He's traveled through time to a different era. He finds himself, with a serious head injury from a fall, at Pearl Harbor Base Hospital on May 16, 1942, three weeks before the Battle of Midway. His wife and aide, Lieutenant Meg Fenton, is worried sick, and waits for him—in 2018.

Admiral Harry is the commanding officer of Carrier Strike Group 14 in 2018, but the people in 1942 think he's a busted-up hallucinating sailor who imagines himself an admiral.

Admiral Raymond Spruance is commanding officer of Carrier Task Force 16. After hearing about Harry's time travel stories, Spruance orders him brought to his flagship, the *USS Enterprise.* After Harry tells him about his time travel experiences, Spruance is convinced the man is insane. But after speaking to him at length, Spruance is amazed at Harry's knowledge of naval tactics and strategy. He calls Harry's bluff and orders him to stay aboard the *Enterprise* for her upcoming engagement at the Battle of Midway. By the end of the battle, Spruance is convinced Harry is an admiral, and thinks of him as a friend.

Now Harry needs to figure out how to travel back to 2018, to his carrier command, but most importantly, to the love of his life, Lieutenant Meg. After Harry returns to the present, the Fentons are deployed on Harry's flagship, the *USS Gerald R. Ford.* The ship encounters another wormhole, this one in the ocean. They are transported to 1944 and participate in the Battle of Leyte Gulf.

The book took me 10 months to write. It went through 20 drafts and three rounds with my editors. I did copious research for the book to ensure its historical accuracy. If you enjoy the genre of time travel, I think you will love this book. I got to know my two main characters in the prequel, The Maltese Incident. Harry and Meg are deeply in love but enjoy constant banter and wisecracks. One of my favorite characters, Admiral Ashley Patterson of The Gray Ship, makes an important cameo appearance in The Violent Sea. – RFM

"What a great book. You will love this book. Time travel telling at its best. At the end you will believe it is possible. Russell Moran has crafted a great continuation from The Maltese Incident his character development has continued from the first book throughout this book and possibly beyond. His writing is so detail oriented you will find yourself believing that time travel is not only real but possible. This book was given to me as a gift but it turned out to be one of the greatest gifts I have ever received. You will find that your investment of money and time reading this book to be a great investment. Time and money both well spent." – Mike the Mailman

A Sea of Fear – A Novel of Time Travel – **Book Three of** *The Harry and Meg Series*
https://amzn.to/2GERuSx

You're Five-Star Admiral Harry Fenton, whom President Blake calls the greatest fighting admiral in American history.

Along with your Navy Commander wife, Meg, you lead your carrier strike group against the worst enemy the country has faced since World War II, a small nation that is intent on destroying the world's shipping industry. The seas of the world have become scenes of plunder, pillage, and mass murder.

The President has convinced you to come out of retirement and put an end to the looming crisis. He promotes you to Fleet Admiral, the highest-ranking officer since Admiral William Halsey. You and Meg were having a pleasant retirement, running a world-class resort that you bought in Rhode Island. But when the president pleads you to "Give 'em Hell, Harry," you know that you can't ignore his call to duty.

As people who have time traveled in the past, you come up with an idea to travel three years into the future. With President Blake's blessing, you and Meg lead a group of officers into the future. What you find is horrifying, an America taken over by a totalitarian dictator. You return to the past and report your findings. President Blake, hearing your terrifying story, convinces you that you have an even bigger call to duty, the greatest challenge of your life. You take on the challenge for one reason— Meg will be at your side.

As in the first two books of the Harry and Meg Series, *The Maltese Incident* and *The Violent Sea*, *A Sea of Fear* is a sweet romance between two of literature's most exciting and likable characters, Harry and Meg Fenton. *A Sea of Fear* is a story of war, politics, time travel, and love.

"This story is incredible. I felt like it was real-life and happening NOW! The way the political world is unfolding with the lies and innuendos, something like this could be possible. The main couple, husband and wife, Meg and Harry worked together to solve and help the nation climb onto its rock-solid feet. Surely this is the integrity that the United States government stands for. They had me in their corner wanting to see them win against the evil Antonio Martin. Read the story, it will enthrall and pull you in as it did me...Great ending." – Cristella

The Pineaire Incident **– Book Four of** ***The Harry and Meg Series***
https://amzn.to/2VXQ2lp

One hundred gigantic fast submarines suddenly appear in the ocean. President Harry Fenton and his First Lady, Meg are shocked by the event, as are all the leaders of the world. Where are the submarines from? What do they want? What are their intentions?

Six Russian submarines attack one of the mystery subs. All six Russian subs are destroyed in two minutes.

President Fenton, along with Meg, reaches out to contact the leader of the strange fleet. They are amazed to discover that the subs are from another planet, Planet Pineaire. But they're pleased to find out that the Pinearians came in peace, and bring with them an amazing gift, a new type of fuel that can revolutionize life on earth.

Get ready for an interplanetary thrill ride.

"Right at the beginning, we learn that 100 giant submarines are discovered with no idea how they could all suddenly appear. Being familiar with Harry and Meg, I immediately presumed they must have Time Traveled from some future time. Uh Oh, I almost gave away an important detail. You should already know that Harry and Meg are President and First Lady having recently defeated a small rogue nation that destroyed the Cruise Ship industry and nearly took over the world's Shipping Industry. You might think peaceful times are ahead when abruptly, 100 of these 1,800 foot long submarines appear. Five Stars." – The Holey One

THE DETECTIVING SERIES
Puzzles - **Book One of** *The Detectiving Series*
https://amzn.to/2MI6TEo

Veteran police detectives Bobbie Nelson and Bob Lawton are partnered. They're both concerned that they may not get along. They're both highly skilled and love their work—They love to solve puzzles. They love *Detectiving*. They soon learn that they don't just love their jobs, they love each other. *Detectiving* is an action-packed police thriller wrapped around a sweet romance.

Bobbie and Bob, the BBs, are two of the most exciting and likeable characters you will find in literature.

"This book should be kept out of the hands of crooks, criminals, terrorists, and any others planning to do evil. There are so many techniques utilized by skilled detectives that are revealed that this book could be used as a training guide by the Bad Guys. Even so, the reality is that fundamental police work is what solves most crimes. Gathering and evaluating massive amounts of data and looking for patterns or repeating details is what our two main characters excel at." – The Holey One

"Russell Moran has done it again with "Detectiving." Each case builds upon earlier ones, with the BBs fine-tuning their puzzle-solving techniques to such a degree, it's not long before the FBI and CIA reach out them to piece together more complicated scenarios impacting on society. Russell has created an easy-to-read and fast-paced story, which will keep you turning the pages late into the evening to find out what happens next. I can't wait for the next book in the series!" – R. J. Krzak

Puzzles - **Book Two of** *The Detectiving Series*
https://amzn.to/3bmiqEh

The further adventures of Bobbie Nelson and Bob Lawton, now married. NYPD Detectives First Grade Bobbie Nelson and Bob Layton are partners, husband and wife, and, as Bobbie loves to say, best friends. They both agree that the day they were partnered was the luckiest day of their lives. Police Commissioner Ralph Norquist is their boss and also their good friend. He nicknames them, "the BBs." Norquist discovers that he can assign the most difficult cases to them and they will get the job done. It's almost routine the way they solve child kidnapping cases, serial killer murders, attacks on subway trains, a huge case of drone attacks on football stadiums, and Internet fraud attacks on senior citizens. But what never becomes routine is their love for each other. When they get to their office in the morning, they begin the day with a hug and a kiss. Their partnership almost ended when Bobbie was shot in the head at a crime scene.

She spent six long weeks in a semi-comatose state. Bob said it was the worst six weeks of his life, not knowing if Bobbie would fully recover. Fortunately, the bullet wound did no permanent brain damage, and Bobbie came back to her old self, including her photographic memory. Besides being famous detectives, they're also talented writers. Bob had written a best-selling crime novel before they met, and they both collaborated on a nonfiction book on the art of being a detective - *Detectiving*. That book became a runaway best seller and the royalties poured in. Their book profits, combined with a generous inheritance from Bob's uncle, as well as their combined salaries, made them more than comfortable financially. They renovated their apartment near police headquarters. Bob had bought the building before they met.

After a neighboring tenant moved out. They knocked down a wall and created a 3,000 square foot apartment, a three-block walk from One Police Plaza. Realizing that they need to get away from their hectic work occasionally, they bought a beautiful mansion in East Hampton, and they love to spend weekends there with friends and family—until they discover they are being stalked by a serial killer.

The Long Island Project – **Book Three of** *The Detectiving Series*
https://amzn.to/2WgJC2n

"Another winner!"

Our old friends, Detectives Bobbie Nelson and Bob Lawton, "the BBs," are engaged in the most frightening case of their career, an armed quarantine of Long Island by a sinister group. To find the answer to the problem, they travel through time to 1942, and discover the problem is larger than they had thought.

The third novel in Russell's Patterns Series, we meet up again with the infamous detectives, Bobbie Nelson and Bob Lawson as they're called upon to solve another problem. Why is Long Island under quarantine, and who is behind it? Before long, they uncover a conspiracy, which could lead a takeover through mind control and time travel.

"As with all of Moran's novels, the characters adapt to the situations they find themselves in and their interactions bring the best out in the 'good guys and gals' and will turn readers against those behind the conspiracy. There's plenty of intrigue for everyone as the 'BBs' solve their latest puzzle. I look forward to their next adventure!" – RK

Robot Depot
http://amzn.to/2zXW7C2

Mike Bateman is a visionary businessman, the creator and CEO of the fabulously successful chain of stores, Robot Depot, a company dedicated to selling robots and Artificial Intelligence machines for a variety of uses.

The company is a darling of Wall Street and is the most popular destination for consumers and businesses looking for labor saving devices. But the company caught the eye of ISIS, the terrorist Islamic State. They discover a great way to deliver bombs – using the products of Robot Depot to kill people. Robot Depot changed from being a popular company to an object of fear because of the tampered products it sells. The terrorists use the company for "terror spectaculars," including the destruction of a skyscraper, a drone attack on Yankee Stadium, and the bombing of a children's sailing regatta.

Mike Bateman and the FBI are in a race to stop his products from becoming weapons, a race to stop the wanton killings. His wife and partner, Jenny, discovers the true meaning of terror one horrible summer day.

"Moran just got a new fan. This is the first book of Moran's that I've read, but I look forward to reading more of his work. I enjoyed this story, and found that Moran is not only a good writer, but he's a good storyteller as well. It's an interesting and creative story, mixing new technology and AI uses, with terrorism. It's a thriller that keeps the reader turning the page, and it's extremely captivating. I enjoyed the story and look forward to future works of his." – Amy's Bookshelf

Leonardo Murphy – A Coming of Age Thriller
https://amzn.to/31vzC4S

You just launched a satellite into space without a rocket. You invented a computer algorithm that writes novels. You just entered Harvard University on a full scholarship after completing high school in two years. Not bad for a 12-year-old kid.

Leonardo changed his name from William to Leonardo to honor his hero, Leonardo da Vinci. Young Leonardo Murphy has the second highest IQ ever recorded. Now 25, he met a beautiful young woman named Janice, and fell madly in love. They married a year later.

Janice and Leonardo, whom she calls "Lee," collaborate on various projects with the CIA and FBI. But their intelligence activities put a target on their backs. They narrowly escape four assassination attempts.

Leonardo Murphy is a breathtakingly fast coming-of-age thriller about one of the most fascinating characters you will ever meet in literature. Instantly, you are shoulder to shoulder with the world's most amazing genius.

"Finally, a believable super hero comes to life! Peaks and valleys of horrific actions are neatly juxtaposed against comic relief. The humor, ranging between the poles of mild to downright hysterical, will surely tickle your funny bone. The frequent use of the protagonist's favorite word (26 matches found throughout), which I won't divulge, would ordinarily belabor one's prose, save when Leonardo employs the term. As a matter of fact, the story concludes with that very word, but rather endearingly. No, I did not ruin the ending for you folks. You'll see." – Robert Banfelder

The Silent Author
https://amzn.to/3cBLRlR

Author Melanie Pierce is widely acknowledged to be the country's greatest novelist. Suddenly she faces the worst form of censorship imaginable – *Editorial Terrorism*. Her words are no longer her own. Before she can publish a book, she, and her fellow authors, must submit the manuscript to a shadowy group of terrorists. Failure to do so will result in the death of one of her loved ones.

A page-turning thriller about a famous page-turning author. Melanie's husband, Max Wakefield, is an FBI agent, and has been assigned to lead what had become known as *The Silent Author Case*. His dedication as an FBI agent, as well as his deep love for his wife, Melanie, launched Max into the most dangerous assignment of his career.

"A thrilling plot shifting page turner about a page turning author." – LK

A Charter Through Time
https://amzn.to/34f9BM4

Former federal prosecutor, Janey Drake, has resigned her legal job because she could no longer put up with the stress of prosecuting drug dealers and the frustrating meanderings of the criminal justice system. She decides to resign after an ironclad case was dismissed by a "caring" judge. She takes on a new life that she loves, chartering her 60-foot yacht that was a gift from her wealthy father. An experienced large boat captain, Janey has found a cure for the high stress work of her former occupation. She also found a cure for her loneliness when she met the man of her dreams by a chance encounter in a diner. Jack Fleming is a famous novelist and loves his work, and soon finds out that he loves Janey, his accidental friend from the diner. He and Janey fall impossibly in love with each other and found a way to blend their lives—cruising the high seas and writing about it. Janey has taken on the role as Jack's editor and she couldn't be happier.

But suddenly their happy lives together take on a frightening new dimension. While cruising off New London, Connecticut, their boat encounters a wormhole or time portal, and they find themselves two years into the future, a horrifying future that had seen a nuclear war. They find out that their apartment building in Manhattan was the target for one of the bombs. Yes, they discover that they had been killed, two years ago. But yet they're alive. Time travel is a strange phenomenon, and sometimes a scary one.

They realize that they have no choice. They must return to the past and warn the government about the coming horror.

They begin the most terrifying experience of their lives—how to go back in time and prevent your own death, and the deaths of millions of others.

"A time-travel mind bender." – LK

The Love We Almost Lost
https://amzn.to/2G8iMnR

Regulations frown upon a military doctor being romantically involved with a patient.

But Lieutenant Rebecca Lang, a Navy physician, frowned upon the regulations. She fell madly in love with Captain Jack Parker, a wounded Marine officer under her care at Bagram Airbase in Afghanistan.

Doctor Rebecca, or Becca as she prefers to be called, felt that she had a rare bond with Captain Jack. It began as a simple doctor-patient relationship, then developed into a friendship, then, after constant flirting, it became a serious love affair. Captain Jack was happy that Becca ignored the regulations, and so was she.

When they were discharged from the military within two weeks of each other, they looked forward to making their relationship permanent, and planned to marry. But, on the day Jack returned to the States, he was mugged, and suffered a multi-year mental blackout from amnesia. Becca didn't know where he was, and she assumed he was dead after such a long absence. Becca sees Jack interviewed on TV, although the man doesn't think he's Jack because he suffers from severe amnesia. When they meet, Jack comes out of his amnesia and his mind remembers the woman his heart had never forgotten. They resume their love and their lives together. Becca, widely recognized as the nation's expert on infectious diseases, is tapped by the White House to combat a deadly virus that has been set loose on the world.

Jack, who by now has become an FBI Agent, joins his wife Becca in the most terrifying struggle they ever experienced—the fight to save humanity.

THE WORMHOLE ADVENTURES
The Wormhole Gang – Book 1 of *The Wormhole Adventures*
https://amzn.to/3nTxLlN

"Jack, where the hell are we?"

Admiral Ashley Patterson, the Navy's youngest admiral at age 39, was with her husband, famous publisher Jack Thurber. Jack is a commander in the Naval Reserve, and often accompanies

Ashley on assignments. They were on their most enjoyable deployment to date. Ashley had been given command of the famous *USS Intrepid*, an aircraft carrier that had become a museum, a three-month post that was largely ceremonial. The Navy's thinking was that Ashley's new command would be an excellent way to promote the museum, as well as a great public relations stunt for the Navy. Both history lovers, they were enjoying Ashley's latest assignment—until they came to face with the most horrifying situation they ever encountered.

One early morning they awoke, expecting to see themselves alongside Pier 86. Instead, they were shocked to see that they were in the middle of the ocean. While they slept, the ship, without an engine or other discernible source of power, suddenly left its dock on the West Side of Manhattan—with nobody at the controls. They realized that the ship had gone through a time portal, a wormhole.

They were lost at sea—and lost in time.

Along with two other crew members, they formed a group to discover what had happened to them. Admiral Ashley named the group *The Wormhole Gang*.

"This book takes time travel to a wild new level. I feel like I know the characters personally." – JC Prince.

About the Author

In addition to the 25 novels discussed above, I also published five nonfiction books: *Justice in America: How it Works – How it Fails; The APT Principle: The Business Plan That You Carry in Your Head; Boating Basics: The Boattalk Book of Boating Tips; If You're Injured: A Consumer Guide to Personal Injury Law; How to Create More Time.* My latest nonfiction book is *The Novel – A Writer's Guide – Discover the Joy of Writing Fiction.* I'm a lawyer and a veteran of the United States Navy. I live on Long Island, New York, with my wife and editor, Lynda, and a Golden Retriever named Maggie. Maggie makes a cameo appearance in many of my books.

A Personal Request

I hope you enjoyed reading *The Wormhole Crisis* as much as I enjoyed writing it. Ashley and Jack are two of my favorite characters. You may recall reading about them in *The Gray Ship*, *The Thanksgiving Gang, The Skies of Time* and *The Keepers of Time.* I think of them as old friends. Ashley is now a Fleet Admiral and Chairwoman of the Joint Chiefs of Staff. As always, Jack is by her side. You will be seeing more of them in future books.

Please consider leaving a brief review of *The Wormhole Crisis* on amazon.com. Open this link: **https://amzn.to/37yzTu4**

It doesn't need to be lengthy or elaborate, just your thoughts on the characters, the scenes, and the story. Book reviews are the lifeblood of an author.

I Deeply thank you.

Russ Moran